Hood Consigliere

Keese

Lock Down Publications and Ca$h
Presents

Hood Consigliere
A Novel by *Keese*

Keese

Lock Down Publications
Po Box 944
Stockbridge, Ga 30281

Visit our website @
www.lockdownpublications.com

Lock Down Publications
Like our page on Facebook: Lock Down Publications @
www.facebook.com/lockdownpublications.ldp
Book interior design by: **Shawn Walker**
Edited by: **Tamira Butler**

Hood Consigliere

Stay Connected with Us!

Text **LOCKDOWN** to 22828 to stay up-to-date with new releases, sneak peaks, contests and more...
Thank you.

Submission Guideline.

Submit the first three chapters of your completed manuscript to ldpsubmissions@gmail.com, subject line: Your book's title. The manuscript must be in a .doc file and sent as an attachment. Document should be in Times New Roman, double spaced and in size 12 font. Also, provide your synopsis and full contact information. If sending multiple submissions, they must each be in a separate email.

Have a story but no way to send it electronically? You can still submit to LDP/Ca$h Presents. Send in the first three chapters, written or typed, of your completed manuscript to:

LDP: Submissions Dept
Po Box 944
Stockbridge, Ga 30281

DO NOT send original manuscript. Must be a duplicate.

Provide your synopsis and a cover letter containing your full contact information.

Thanks for considering LDP and Ca$h Presents.

Keese

Prologue

High above in the sky, the moon illuminated a clear, dark filled area, as a gentle breeze below caressed the land.

All of the streets in the overpopulated ghettos of Durham, North Carolina on such a night were rarely deserted. Old, moderate houses and tall, thick trees lined the streets. One of those houses, a white one trimmed in black, with only a few lights on inside, was being used to conceal an illegal business from the view of public eyes.

Inside the house, drug dealers pushed and peddled massive amounts of coke by the weight, as if they were selling white bricks to help build a church in their community. Even though it was fairly late in the night, more money could have been generated if the pushers had more product to sell on demand.

"Yo, Rock! Niggas is crazy, man. They always want a nigga to cook their shit too. Next, they'll be asking us to smoke test for them," Mellow said humorously. "Shit, pay me, fuck that crazy shit," he spat as the money machine counted a stack of fifty-dollar bills with incredible speed.

"But wouldn't we make more money cooking too," Kasara said more than asked.

Rock looked up and away from the machine. He peered across the room to Kasara for a moment and stared at her hard. She was dark skinned with long hair. Her body was slender and delicate. Her almond-shaped, bright brown eyes seemed to sparkle when she smiled with her full, sensual lips.

But her most dominating features were her extremely large breasts. Rock was surprised by how erect they sat, considering she wore no bra to support them. "He called Rock, not Kasara! I told you 'bout that shit," he spat with an ill look masking his face. "Wrap that fucking money up and stay out of my business."

She tossed a bundle of bills on the table and looked Rock over as if she was sizing him up, and even though he was much bigger than her, she was not afraid. "You keep talking to me like that, yo' ass will be sleeping on the floor tonight," she said, rolling her eyes wildly in defiance.

"I don't know why you playing, girl. You know you gonna want some just as soon as y'all leave," her sister Denise said in an attempt to stop an argument from starting.

"So, stop all that messing. Hurry up wrapping that money so I can go. You know I hate being in this house when y'all doing this shit," she added.

"You shouldn't have come then," her boyfriend Mellow yelled. "You always coming over here with that water-head shit. You know what this house is for… always complaining. But you ain't got jack to say when you spending the money. Talking 'bout what you hate."

Mellow and Denise had been dating off and on over a short period of time. Soon after meeting him, her sister, Kasara, soon took a liking to his friend, Rock. That was a year ago and from that day, both sisters remained loyal, known drug dealers throughout the heart of Durham.

Money brought happiness in their world, and that itself held them together like Crazy Glue, through thick and thin.

Denise stood momentarily in silence, hands on hips, unsure of what to say. "It's just that my sister and I have been counting money all day at work, then we come here and help y'all count drug money. We would, for once, like to spend some real quality time with y'all for just one day and not have to count money," she said softly.

Her soft-spoken words hit Mellow at heart. "Okay, how 'bout we go out tomorrow for dinner," he said, walking across the room, pulling on a gangster-sized blunt.

"And I'll pick the spot," Rock added.

The twin sisters looked the men up and down, as if they were thinking from the same brain. "That's what you said the last time!" Denise shouted across the room, challenging Mellow.

"I forgot… but this time, I won't," he said. Mellow walked across the room, stopping inches in front of her.

They both held a locking gaze, like lovers in bed. Slowly, Mellow licked his lips then blew smoke into the air. "I'm sorry, baby. Can I make it up to you?" He leaned closely to her ear. "I'll eat that pussy for ya," he whispered lightly into her ear.

Suddenly, Kasara noticed a wicked smile appear on her sister's face.

"What he say?" she asked.

"He's over here talking about French kissing me," Denise responded in only a language her sister could decipher.

"Ooowww!" Kasara said with her mouth wide open, lips forming the letter O. "I knew you was a freak, girl!"

"You are too!" Rock added, exposing Kasara's little secret. "So don't even play like you ain't." Kasara smiled lightly, knowing he was right.

"So, where we going and when?" Kasara asked, directing the question at both men.

"How about tomorrow, we fly to the Bahamas?" Rock added. Kasara folded her arms across her chest with a surprised look on her face.

"Girl, this fool is crazy. He knows damn well they not taking us to no Bahamas. Shit! Hell, we can't even get them to take our black asses to a movie, and the theater is right here."

"No, I'm not," Rock said. "If you or your sister call the airline and make the reservations, we straight."

As Kasara called American Airlines to arrange reservations for the flight, Mellow, Rock, and Denise returned to counting, wrapping, and stacking money. They were all excited about the trip. This would be more than a trip for the twins. They were already off work for the upcoming week, so for them, this trip would be an unforgettable vacation.

The sisters knew they would be very busy the next day. Shopping, beauty salon, manicure, pedicure, etc., etc. Kasara was on the phone, sounding overly excited as she peered around and observed everyone working. Two money machines were the only sound heard, besides that of her voice. Mellow placed stacks of money into duffle bags lined up on a nearby table.

Moments later, she hung up the phone. "Aight y'all, we have a plane to catch tomorrow at 8:00 p.m."

Suddenly, a loud, frightening crashing sound came from an unknown place within the house. Mellow quickly jumped to his feet

11

and pulled his gun out. Rock dove to the floor and aimed his pistol down the hall.

A large man, about five feet ten, appeared suddenly in the hallway with a Wu-Tang mask wrapping portions of his face, concealing his identity. The intruder was dressed from head to toe in graveyard black army fatigues and a black bulletproof vest. Dump pouches equipped with extra clips for a military style AR-15 circled his waist. Another slightly smaller figure appeared directly beside him, raising and aiming a .45 caliber in each hand.

Rock aimed his gun at the target. He pulled back on the trigger and let off two hotshots, completely missing his intended target. The large intruder jerked his head left as slugs exploded sheet rock from the wall. He returned fire with his AR-15 over and over, as slugs and hot, bright flashes escaped his barrel with a strobe light effect. Kasara dove to the floor as soon as the thunderous shots rang out.

She screamed loudly as Rock's body jerked from the impact of the bullets.

Just as quickly as the gunfire started, it suddenly ended. "Shut the fuck up, bitch!" yelled one of the gunmen.

"And drop that gun, nigga," he yelled at Mellow, "before you join your man. The next motherfucker in here that moves even a muscle is gonna die."

Once both gunmen had everyone on the floor, the shorter intruder kneeled down and slapped Mellow back and forth violently in the face with his barrel, as if he was trying to knock plaque loose from his teeth. "Aight, you better listen up," he began with a wicked voice. "When I ask a question, you better nod your head yes or no, you got me?"

"Yeah," Mellow said.

The intruder slapped him across his face disrespectfully with his barrel. "Nigga, what the fuck I tell your dumb ass? I said no talking, faggot."

Mellow was bleeding heavily from a cut above his eye. "Now let's do this one more time. Is there any money in here?" Mellow nodded yes.

As the shorter intruder questioned Mellow, the larger one removed a roll of duct tape from his shirt pocket and taped everyone's wrists, ankles, and mouths. Moments later, he packed loose money into the duffle bags on the table. To his surprise, it appeared to be about a quarter of a million dollars in large bills.

He went back into the living room just as his partner finished putting money into his duffle bag. "Aight," the intruder yelled for all to hear as he walked over toward the females, removing his knife. "Bitch, shut the fuck up. I'm only going to cut you loose. If I wanted to kill you, Denise, your pretty ass would be dead by now."

He leaned in, towering over the woman, and cut through the duct tape on her wrists. "When we leave, you should be able to work that loose and free the others," he informed her, "and if any one of you even peeks out the door when we gone, I'll come back and kill you all," he swore.

Heartbeats later, both men exited the house with stealth movements like thieves moving into darkness. Everyone on the floor looked on helplessly in disbelief, relieved to still have their lives intact, knowing they could have been killed. Denise frantically worked on the duct tape until she freed herself. After removing the tape from her mouth, she sprinted to the kitchen, returning moments later with a knife to cut the others free.

"Y'all okay?" Mellow asked with concern as he stood up.

"Them bastards killed my sweetheart," Kasara screamed, devastated by his sudden death but relieved that they were spared. Kasara yelled loudly, crying, "No, no!"

As Denise embraced hear in an attempt to comfort her, she knew that soothing words would never replace her sister's boyfriend or bring him back.

"Them two niggas killed my best friend. Them niggas gonna die," Mellow swore to both of them. "Denise, do you know them?" Mellow asked.

Denise stared at Mellow with an expression of shock. "No, why would I know who they are?" she asked, fanatically crying.

"One of them called your name," he informed her. "I'ma find out who they are. Durham is not all that big that I can't find out.

Niggas kick my door in and jack me like that. When I do find out," he said, looking Denise in the eyes, "I'ma kill them."

Chapter 1

Early the very next morning, Sunami and Shadow both sat on plush, white, Italian leather sofas. Both were leaning back, heads slightly tilted upward, pulling back hard on their third cognac-flavored Royal blunts filled with hydro. Together they'd been watching *Shotas* on a larger than life-size television hanging from the ceiling.

Although both men lived a hard knock life, they were men of great taste and were into designer clothes, diamonds, luxurious cars, and exotic women. They lived like celebrities.

They held not a care in the world when it came to spending money. "Why work hard when others could slave for you until you collect?" was their long-term motto. They agreed a long time ago that robbing the next man was no different than an IRS officer in a black man's world collecting taxes.

Sunami peered around his living room and felt grateful his life had been spared in all his years of selling drugs and pulling off stick-ups. With every heartbeat, flirting with death was similar to a gangster toying with Satan himself.

He nonchalantly removed both feet from his granite and glass coffee table, placing them flat on a thick black oriental rug. He reached down and retrieved his universal remote, which was right beside the pound of hydro he and Shadow were smoking from.

He aimed the device and pressed a sequence of buttons with his thumb. A nanosecond later, music from a surround sound system pounded with thunderous bass from speakers, six-feet high, positioned in the corners of the room.

"Man, lower that loud ass shit," Shadow shouted in an attempt to be heard over the music. "Heart of the City" by Jay-Z blasted over murderous beats. Sunami thought he witnessed Shadow's lips moving; however, he was unsure.

"What? You say something?"

"Man, we should do something today, like go out of town or something," suggested Shadow.

"Last night, after we robbed Mellow and Rock, I was thinking about going to the 4.0 to see our boy, Outlaw. Whatcha think?" Sunami responded while blowing smoke in the air.

"That crazy motherfucker?" Shadow laughed.

"Sounds good to me. And you know he knows all the pussy spots up there."

"Yo, remember that bitch Juicy. She had a mean jaw bone on her and a fat ass. Now she healthy as hell," Sunami said.

"Yeah, and she had you open too," Shadow said, tormenting him with a laugh.

"Fuck you, man, ain't shit when Carmen had you open," Sunami said and began laughing. "The first time she gave you head; you went and bought her a brand-new BMW. Shit, you were the one open, so don't even hate, nigga."

"Nah, cousin, I got her that shit because I crashed her car while she was giving me head," Shadow said in his own defense, lying.

"Whatever, nigga," Sunami shot back with laughter, while walking across the room to a table filled with stolen money from last night's take. He picked up the phone, dialed a number, and waited for someone to pick up on the other end. He mashed his blunt out in an ashtray.

"Yo, what's up?" someone answered with a New York accent, sounding as if he just woke up.

"What up, Outlaw, what you doing today?" Sunami said.

"First of all, who questioning me?" Outlaw asked defensively.

"This your cousin, Sunami, fool. Me and Shadow thinking about coming up and chilling with you for the weekend."

"Yo, what the deal, son?" Outlaw asked, sounding excited. "Damn, it's been a minute. So, what's popping down south, kid?"

"Me and Shadow was thinking about driving up to see you, but I wanted to call you up first to check if you'll be home."

"No question, I'll be home. Shit, I was catching forty winks until your ass woke me up."

"You always sleeping."

"Nigga, you would be too if yo' country ass rested in the city that never sleeps. You know me, son, I fuck all day and all night.

Hood Consigliere

What's wrong with that, I don't need paper. Got enough of that shit to hold me, on some real shit."

Hearing the word money, Sunami quickly thought back to last night's take and began explaining things to his cousin… in so many words.

Both men conversated back and forth for about fifteen minutes or so, discovering there was so much they needed to catch up on, and couldn't wait to see one another again. Moments later, Sunami and Shadow packed a few things, got dressed, ate, and rolled a few blunts for their trip to Yonkers. Sunami and Shadow pulled onto the highway heading north in the heavy morning traffic.

"Don't be doing no ninety-five in a sixty-five either. I know how you get at times," Sunami said from the passenger seat. An accident was up ahead blocking a lane, causing traffic to slow to a crawl.

Shadow slowed the car down to a normal speed when he saw the flashing police lights ahead in the distance.

"The only time I speed is when it is absolutely necessary. Other than that, I don't speed. You the one who be speeding and—"

"It's my ride, that's why!" Sunami interjected, cutting him off, laughing as he crunched his blunt out in the ashtray while lowering the window.

"We cool?" Shadow said seriously.

"Yeah, we cool, but you know what to do if anything happens," Sunami responded. He then removed a gun from his hideaway hip holster and chambered a round for added protection against prison time.

Both men continued moving about in the car as if they had been law-fearing citizens since childhood.

As they passed two cops directing traffic, Shadow's heart skipped a beat out of fear of being pulled over. Both men hated police with a passion.

Just a few yards up ahead, traffic was being detoured to an off-ramp, over the bridge to an on-ramp. As they exited the highway, both men noticed an eighteen-wheeler jack-knifed across the highway, blocking two lanes of traffic.

17

"Whatcha sweating for?" Shadow asked, turning back onto the highway after crossing the bridge.

"I'm always sweating when I'm about to bust a cap in a motherfucker's ass," Sunami responded while sliding his pistol back into its holster. "Speaking of sweating, did you notice that crazy ass stunt that nigga attempted last night trying to shoot me? Man, I lit his ass up. Now that's how you body a motherfucker. Dude wasn't trying to come off that money, so now he's dead because of stupidity, and we still got the money."

"Some niggas will die for anything, you know how that goes," Shadow responded.

"And you... what the fuck you call that stupid bitch Denise name for? Now that was stupid, man. You know we can't be doing no shit like that. You got to stay on point with that. You hear me?"

Shadow shrugged his shoulders. "That bitch got me heated. I wanted to kill that no-good bitch... her pretty ass. You think she'll say anything?"

"Nah... I don't, and so what if she does."

"She and them Southside niggas can get it! For her own safety, if she does know, she better not say shit. Snitches get it too."

"But we don't need any careless mistakes. We've come too far, Shadow. So, try and always remain mindful of that shit, aight? So please don't let it happen again, it could cost us next time." Carelessness wasn't a mistake that Sunami took lightly at all, and Shadow knew this since the day they first met each other.

Sunami reflected on their past life as he sat in silence, listening to "Streets Is Watching" by Jay-Z. Twenty-seven-year-old Marcus McKnight, known to everyone as Sunami, was born and raised in the roughest, ruthless, and most dangerous streets of Durham, North Carolina. Shortly after the death of his mother, he underwent a dramatic change and become a self-supporting youth. He did not have the guidance of a father. He quickly turned to the streets, becoming a full-fledged hustler. He did whatever had to be done in order to get money to support himself.

He ascended quickly to the top of the drug game when he met and befriended Dwight Carter, also known as Shadow. Soon they were hated and feared by many but respected at the same time. Both men were ambitious and determined. They accepted no limitation or obstacle and prospered with brute force. Together, they built their own team and devised a strategy to cut out the middleman.

Their team pushed crack throughout the streets of Durham as if a mile-high wave caused by an earthquake hit town. Sunami and Shadow's phenomenal success crushed the old, the new, and up-and-coming drug dealers. And despite Sunami's quiet air of authority, he was murderous. Dealings related to drugs, he accepted as being personal. He became a man of action by way of force, threats, extortion, kidnapping, robbery, and even murder.

Kilo, Tray, Avon, and Homicide, four powerful local drug dealers, vanished mysteriously, never seen or heard from again. Word spread around town like tuberculosis that Sunami played a major role in their disappearance. Though true, his involvement was never proven. His position of power allowed him to do and get away with just about anything.

All the champagne-sipping, chunky diamond earring-sporting and Rolex-wearing, player-hating wannabes couldn't wait to reach the status of power he had. With a mix of admiration and envy in their hearts, they wanted what he had. It was also no secret that most wanted him dead, or brought down, so they could step in his place.

Keese

Chapter 2

"So, let's get this straight, or should I say, correct?" a large man behind an even larger mahogany desk asked.

"Two guys kicked in your door last night while you and Rock were counting my money and robbed you? Is that what you telling me, Mellow?"

"Yes, sir," he responded in a firm tone of voice while lighting a cigarette.

"It happened so fast, there was nothing we could do," he continued while blowing smoke high into the air. "Rock shot at one them, and the dude shot back. He shot Rock in the chest and the head. Cuba, there was nothing we could do."

Suddenly, Cuba jumped to his feet. "What the fuck you mean, you couldn't do anything? Then why the fuck you here telling me some shit about my money getting stolen? You should be searching every damn house on the face of the earth for what's mine!"

"I'll find it, sir."

"You bet your ass you will! Where's Rock's body now?" Cuba asked, sounding a bit calmer.

"Me and a friend took care of it. I thought it was best we didn't involve the cops. That would put more heat on us than I can handle right now."

"Good thinking, at least you did something correct." Cuba took a seat back behind the desk. "What all did they get?"

"A little over a quarter million, can't say for sure exactly how much they…"

Cuba noticed Mellow's hesitation. "They what?"

Mellow was about to reveal that he and Rock had their girlfriends over, which was a grave mistake. "I was about to say the money machine was still counting hundreds at the time they busted in on us. We had some bills left to count."

"Umm hmm. Did you recognize either of them?" he asked, lighting a cigar.

"Well, to be completely honest with you, there was one that reminded me of this guy named Sunami I went to school with, kinda moved like him. A few people told me that he and this other dude named Shadow specialize in home invasions."

"I've heard of them. I think they once kicked in a door of one of my other houses a few years back and came off with close to a hundred fifty thousand. Killed everyone inside the house, so we couldn't prove it. Let's find that son of a bitch." Cuba picked up the phone, dialed, and waited for Mario to answer. "Mario, take one of the cars, round up three guys, and search the streets until you find a guy named Sunami. He's our man on last night's take, so I need this one alive. Any problems, just shoot him in the kneecaps, understand?"

"What about a family member if we can't locate this guy?"

"Do whatever it takes. Nobody takes from Cuba and lives long enough to enjoy it." He slammed down the phone and peered over at Mellow. "I don't want you saying one word to anyone about this. Continue working as if nothing happened. Don't even speak about this with your friends. I'll handle this one…understand?"

"Yeah."

Cuba stood five feet seven inches tall, with short hair sprinkled with gray at the temples. His dark gray, piercing eyes penetrated the soul of anyone that dared to stare into them. He built his network of drug selling from the ground up by employing a team of workers and a death squad of hit men for protection. His enterprise blossomed into the most lucrative money-getting business to hit Durham. Cocaine came into the city by the truckloads, no less than thirty tons a year. His cocaine was pushed out into the streets by weight or dubs. People bought his crack at cheaper rate than the regular price of fifteen to twenty dollars, and it guaranteed an intense high that lasted far longer than any other crack around.

The money generated from street sales of the drug came quickly. It was all COD (cash on delivery). No credit and no shorts. The twenty-dollar grams sold to those who snorted promised fourteen to nineteen lines of pleasure.

Cuba was not a man to be handled lightly. He alone was responsible for the murders of numerous judges throughout the country. Many others felt his wrath, journalists, police officers, members of

SWAT teams, and civilians. He and his monstrous team of killers held no respect for anyone or anything. Only money really mattered.

A lot of time had been invested into his business and security team of henchmen, who were always ready to engage in bloodthirsty battles. His empire included three of the Raleigh-Durham-Chapel Hill area's largest nightclubs, two upscale restaurants, twenty crack houses, and ten heroin spots. Dozens of policemen, attorneys, and judges were on his payroll. There was no doubt in Mellow's mind that Cuba would get Sunami. He owned the police in the Bull City.

Cuba stood in silence for a moment while puffing his cigar. "So, tell me, did you happen to notice anyone suspicious standing around the house?"

"No, I didn't. Why do you ask?" Mellow responded.

"Because if this Sunami is the man we're looking for, then he would've been watching my place for a good length of time to know what kind money was there. Either that, or someone's been running their mouth." Cuba stood up and walked around his desk toward the bar. "You never struck me as one who mouths off about business." He poured himself a glass of scotch. "At least not my business. You see, cause if you were talking, you'd be at the bottom of a lake someplace until the fish are down there feeding on you. So that means this Sunami guy, or whoever he's working with, has been watching my place."

Mellow had no idea where the conversation was heading. "I know what he looks like. I haven't seen him around though."

"How can you be so sure? I doubt you even paid any attention to your surroundings with a fully conscious mind." For a short moment, their eyes locked. "But that's since you've been counting my money and selling my product."

"That's all I've been doing, sir!"

"Sure! I don't think you would try to rip me off. You're not that foolish, and that's what I admire about you, Mellow." He sipped his drink, and the room fell silent for a moment.

"No, sir, I wouldn't be trying to pull such a foolish stunt. I completely respect you. You been feeding me and my family for the past four years and giving me nice vacations."

Cuba walked around the room, making his way back to the desk. Gently, he sat back in his seat.

"You're a nice, bright young kid. You should have a nice bird's nest by now, enough funds to support you and your whole family. But don't let the money cause you to lose focus on what's important in life." He stared intensely into Mellow's eyes while slowly inhaling the cigar smoke.

Mellow thought about Denise and how much she meant to him. She told him she was pregnant with his child.

Deep down within his heart, his family was most important to him.

Suddenly, the phone rang. Cuba picked it up and placed it to his ear. "Okay, sure!" he said. "On my way then." He hung up the phone and looked over at Mellow.

"Hate to be running, but something of great importance has just been brought to my attention. We'll talk more later, okay?"

"Yes, sir, that's fine with me." Mellow was elated that the conversation came to an end. "I need to get a move on myself. Got to pay bills before it gets too late." He glanced at his wristwatch, as if he was really serious. "In the meantime, if anything develops, I'll be sure to give you a holla."

"That's good! Because I'm sure you, Denise, and her sister want this bastard as much as I do. And I assure you, we all will enjoy killing Sunami slowly."

Mellow's eyes flashed with a quizzical look. How the hell did he know about Denise and Kasara? He was sure he never mentioned they were there.

"You okay, son?" Cuba asked.

"Sure, I was just thinking about something."

"We'll talk later," Cuba stated as they walked toward the door.

Chapter 3

After a lengthy nine-hour drive from North Carolina, Sunami and Shadow finally reached the Bronx.

Sunami was behind the wheel and exited off the New England throughway, went round and under an overpass, and turned left onto Baychester Avenue. As he piloted down the busy street, Jay-Z's "Girls, Girls, Girls" blasted with forcefulness throughout the car's trunk. Both gangsters mouthed every word of the track while violently nodding their heads simultaneously to each beat.

Sunami slipped through the traffic like a boxer dodging punches, all in an attempt to get closer to his target.

"Did you see that?" Shadow suddenly asked. He peered at Sunami with a raised eyebrow and quickly lowered the volume.

"See what?" Sunami responded.

"That bitch back there." Shadow pointed back to the street corner they just passed.

"Man, I don't see jack. Where she at?" he asked, peering into his side-view mirror. "Aight, I see her now."

"She thick, right?" Shadow said.

"Hell yeah, that's pussy eating fine too! Man, we gonna do a lot of fucking here, just like we did last month," Sunami swore, slowing his car short of a red light, braking ahead of time behind an all-black Pathfinder with New Jersey tags. He peered down at the fuel indicator. It registered at the one-quarter mark. "We gotta fill up, tank 'bout empty."

"Shit, my stomach the one 'bout empty. Fucking hydro got me hungry as hell," Shadow said. Street corners later, they pulled into a self-service gas station and stopped alongside the premium pump. Sunami and Shadow both got out of the car and stretched.

"You want to fill it up while I walk over there and grab something for us to grub on?" Sunami asked Shadow, pointing to a McDonald's across the busy street.

"How you doing, North Carolina?" a soft, low voice exclaimed. When Sunami realized he was being approached by a woman, he immediately removed the gangster persona from his face and presented what he felt was a more suitable face for such an occasion. He spun around to face the woman. "I'm doing so-so," he responded, instantly gazing into the most irresistible almond-shaped eyes, caressing her body from head to toe, taking in every detail of her beauty.

Jet-black hair cascaded down her shoulders, stopping mid-back, accentuating the smooth texture of her butterscotch complexion. Her full, evenly contoured lips were lightly covered with a glossy, wheat-colored lipstick that afforded her a goddess-like radiance. Her smile showed off perfectly even and white teeth, which made it hard for Sunami to believe they were actually real.

Her breasts were larger than life, standing erect and firm. She stood with her legs slightly apart, dressed in a caramel leather and faux-python jacket and dark denim jeans that stretched around her curvaceous body so tightly that she appeared to be sealed to preserve great taste. Her legs were well defined with perfect muscle tone. He noticed the caramel leather and faux-python boots that stopped only inches below her knees. His eyes moved up her legs, and he suddenly gazed at their perfect V-shape where her inner thighs connected. The thought of those legs wrapped around his neck was so intriguing.

Trying to regain control of the flash of desire that shot through his loins, he continued to stare, silently mesmerized by this woman's beauty. "Well, I can't complain myself," she answered with a warm, melodious voice.

Sunami was simply dressed in a brown and beige jacket, t-shirt, jeans, and Timberland boots. She noticed underneath the fabric of his shirt the thick muscles of his chest, shoulders, arms, and neck. His recent haircut afforded him a look much younger than his twenty-seven years.

He was nicely trimmed and groomed with a platinum diamond-encrusted chain hanging around his neck.

"So, is that your name, Sunami?" she asked, looking at the tattoo on his neck.

"Yes," he answered. Her breasts had him mesmerized. "And your name would be?"

"Oh! Excuse me for my rudeness. My name is Hypnotic," she answered.

"I know you kidding, right? Is that Ms. or Mrs. Hypnotic?"

"It's Ms., for now." When she spoke, the aroma of mint filled the air between them. Sunami noticed her eyes roaming up and down his body, pausing in places longer than they should.

"Are you from this part of town?" Sunami replied.

"No, I'm new to this area. I moved here from Brooklyn 'bout a week ago," she said, while moving closer to him. "So, are you visiting family?" she asked.

"Yes. A cousin of mine lives in Yonkers."

"Oh, I see," she said while gazing at him.

"Me and my sidekick, Shadow, are on our way out there. We're here for the weekend," he said, as he pointed toward the direction of his friend. She turned her upper body slightly to peer over her shoulder and waved at Shadow. She looked again at the milky white model 360 Modena, Ferrari two-seater drop top, sitting on 22-inch polished chrome wheels and the burgundy interior trimmed in white stitching that caught her attention to begin with.

"When I first saw you, I thought you were a loud-mouth, skirt-chasing gangster. But I never seen a thug pushing a $200,000 rocket through a concrete jungle," she moaned. There was light laughter between the two as passersby whistled at her. "So, what kind of work do you do?" she asked.

"I run a large business enterprise," he shot back, somewhat side-stepping the question. "What line of work are you in?" Sunami asked.

"Right now, I'm unemployed. I used to be a schoolteacher, but our yearly income was cut by the Board of Education to balance the budget," she said, lying.

Sunami's cell phone rang. "Can you please excuse me for a second?" he said while reaching for his phone.

While he was speaking on the phone, she reached into her purse and pulled out a pen and a piece of paper and wrote down her number. "Give me a call, when you can," she whispered, being sure not to be heard by whomever he was speaking to.

He nodded and smiled as he accepted her phone number. She turned and walked off very seductively, heading across the street. Her ass looked four months pregnant. Sunami's stare was fixed on it like a security camera as she walked across the busy street. She was the prime example of the fruit of immortality. Even Shadow and those around on the street turned to watch this sexy creature walk away.

"Motherfucker, that bitch is bad, and thick as a son of a bitch!" Shadow yelled across the top of the car. "Damn, did you see that ass? Bitch got booty for days, nice big ol' horse ass! I know you gonna fuck her, right?" Shadow asked excitedly.

Sunami looked at his friend with a puzzled stare.

"Man, fuck that defected pussy. She was full of G-man. When you ever see a teacher dressed like a hooker?" he asked, tossing the number to the ground. "That bitch ain't nothing but a nut rag."

"Man, how you know that? Maybe she wasn't gaming you," Shadow said as he peeled twenty-dollar bills from the folded money in his hand. "Shit, if you thought like that when you were kicking it, why front like you run a large enterprise like Bill Gates?" Both men laughed.

"I was kicking that shit, right! The first thing she noticed was what I'm driving, kid. She's a money-hungry hood rat. I need a career kind of woman in my life. I got a daughter, and her crackhead mama ain't doing shit. So, when I get full custody, I need my daughter to be around a real woman who can teach her how to be a lady in them streets, not a ho. Feel me?" Sunami said, making a point in one breath.

"Yeah! Whatever. I'ma go hit these niggas off for this gas while you go get grub."

"Yeah, what you want, Mr. Will Fuck Anything?"

"Get me a Big Mac, nah two, and an apple pie," Shadow said while walking off toward the store.

"Aight, I'll be back in a minute. Don't let one of these fools jack you for my car," he yelled, knowing Shadow had a gun concealed in his waistline underneath his black hoody.

Sunami entered McDonald's. He couldn't believe how packed it was. All four counters held lines longer than the drive-thru window. Standing in line for a long time was not his thing. He glanced toward the front of the line at a heavyset, big-hipped black woman with round eyes and two small children. She had two chins, weighed at least 250 pounds, and looked about fifty years old. He walked toward her and asked with a charming but false smile, "Excuse me, beautiful, are these your kids?" The woman looked at him strangely.

"No, they are my grandchildren. Why?" she asked, sounding defensive.

"Because I'm in a rush and I would really like to get in and out, if it's no problem with you."

"Well, you can, all you have to do is go back there," he said, pointing toward the end of the line.

Feeling embarrassed, he reached into his front pocket and slowly removed a wad of money that held the bills folded over in place. He quickly removed a few bills. "Will this help you cooperate with me, ma'am?" he asked, flashing four ten-dollar bills before her eyes.

"Well, I can wait a few extra minutes," she said softly, with a smile on her face.

"Thank you very much," he said, handing her the bills. Just as she took the bills and stuffed them into her bra, he saw Hypnotic walking out through the doors.

However, she was not alone. A guy was walking alongside her with his arm around her neck.

"May I help you, sir?" a young woman asked for the second time.

He spun around suddenly at the sound of her voice. "Yes! Can you please give me four Big Macs, two apple pies, and two large drinks, orange, please." After paying and receiving his order, he walked out into the parking lot. He looked around the car to get in on the passenger side.

Keese

"Yeah, I saw that hot-ass bitch, too, with another nigga. Told you she was a hood rat. Fuck her." Sunami pulled out of the parking lot, blending into traffic as DMX shouted "Whatcha bitches want from a nigga" through the speakers.

Chapter 4

Sunami's eyes took in the landscape as he drove his Ferrari down the highway, deeper into Westchester County.

Billboards advertising music, radio stations, clothing, cars, and banks whizzed by the corner of his eyes as he passed exit after exit. Overhead, green and white signs showed what city, town, and exit was about to come up. His attention turned to the mile marker posts and speed limit signs. He glanced at his speedometer. It read: 105 MPH.

He then let up on the accelerator, slowing the car down to 55 MPH. He flipped the right turn signal and switched lanes, pulling up behind red tailgate lights on the car directly in front of him. He almost missed his exit. He hit the right turn signal and exited, almost seconds too late.

"Aight, nigga, keep on driving fast. Fuck around and get pulled over up here," Shadow said, leaning against the door and peeking into the side-view mirror.

"I wish one of these faggot ass cops would try flagging me. This bitch ain't fast for nothing, and I sure as hell ain't packing for show," Sunami shot back, pulling out a blunt. "Shit, we almost there anyway," he added nonchalantly.

As both men continued to conversate, they passed by many dark brick buildings surrounded by littered sidewalks and overturned trash cans. The night view above was gunsmoke gray, and small children rode their bikes up and down the sidewalk. One kid on a bike much too large for him stopped in front of a fruit stand, swiped an apple, and quickly rode off, as an old man barely able to run tried to chase him. Sunami and Shadow laughed at the up-and-coming thug on the getaway bike.

Finally, they arrived at an apartment building on Riverdale Avenue, known as Riverview Projects. The building traveled the entire block and was sixteen floors high. There were many entry ways into the building. People of all sorts stood around doing what they did best. Cars were parked alongside the walkways with doors open and music blaring loudly. Little girls stood by, begging a local drug dealer who was serving crack rocks to the local heads.

He served one after another as if he was giving out government cheese.

"Man did you see that shorty in them green spandex?" asked Shadow.

Sunami squinted. "Yeah, and she was thick to death. Looks like the rest of them like that too. Grab the weed." Sunami pressed a bottom on the console to open the trunk. "I'll grab the bags."

Sunami unloaded the trunk as Shadow gathered up all the weed and dumped the ashtray on the curb. Once they had everything, both men entered the building, got on the elevator, and headed for the tenth floor in search of Outlaw's apartment. The exited the elevator and walked the lengthy hallway to Outlaw's door.

Loud music could be heard in the hallway.

Moments after Sunami pounded on the door, it swung open violently. "What up, my nigga?" Outlaw said, giving them ghetto handshakes. "You niggas ready to party or what? I got bitches in my living room gettin' it on, and they ain't leaving 'til six in the morn'."

"Man, you still the same. Who you got up in here?"

Shadow asked as they entered the apartment and headed for the living room. Sunami looked around and noticed weed, unfilled blunts, and two half gallons of Hennessy on the coffee table.

Outlaw walked over to the table and grabbed a bag of pills. He took two of the purple pills from the bag and tossed them both into his mouth. He turned one of the Hennessy bottles up to his head to wash them down. "Some honeys from Mount Vernon. Straight fucking freaks too. I been fucking all day and getting high as a cloud."

Suddenly, a tall, beautiful, ivory-skinned, buxom white girl walked into the living room. She had a round baby face, long hair, grey eyes, and beautiful lips. She stood butt naked, holding an empty glass. "Yo! Outlaw, we need some more ice in there," she said. Her full-figured body was stacked like an Amazon, with ass and breasts that jiggled as she walked. Shadow's body tingled as she walked. Desire and strong anticipation spread through his body like a quick current of electricity.

"Damn!" he said as she walked away, with her ass jumping hypnotically from left to right. "What's her name?"

Shadow asked Outlaw.

"That's un… that bitch named Candy. And got an ill ass blow job on her too."

"Say word?" Shadow asked excitedly.

Candy re-entered the living room with a glass filled with ice. She lightly whispered in Shadow's ear, "Come back to the bedroom and I'll show you the difference between a country girl and a city woman." She stroked his manhood as she stood up. Shadow was unsure of how to respond, and stood for a moment in complete silence. He wanted her in every way.

"Son, y'all can take your things into the next room," Outlaw said, "I'm about to roll some blunts."

"Yeah, you go do that, because I'm about to grab a nice, hot, long shower," Shadow said.

Sunami wondered about the pills in the bag, and he asked Outlaw about them. When Outlaw told him about the ecstasy pills and their effect, he and Shadow each decided to try three. "Nigga, these shits kill me, Irma fuck your short ass up," Sunami said, turning to face Outlaw.

Outlaw was short at about five feet seven, with shoulder-length dreadlocks, a medium-built frame, and a golden complexion. Both men respected Outlaw and all that he believed in because he was known as a solid kind of guy who loved getting high, talking gangster trash, and killing.

Many people thought that after being shot four times in the back that Outlaw would slow down and change his lifestyle. However, he proved them all wrong by killing the guy who shot him.

"Nigga, the day you even think about killing me, I'll chase your big ass directly to hell," Outlaw said as he pulled on a newly rolled blunt. "Trust me, them shits will have you live until Sunday night. You're gonna try to fuck everything walking. That's why white niggas love 'em, cause dem shits keep their little ass dicks hard."

All three men gathered the bags and walked to the empty bedroom. When they got back to the living room, Sunami and Shadow noticed two other females on the sofa laughing and playing with Candy as she pulled hard on a blunt.

"Who's your friend, Outlaw?" asked a doe-eyed, dark-skinned woman with short-cropped hair. Sunami locked eyes with the woman for an instant, quickly looking her up and down. She had large breasts with dark nipples and full, sturdy hips.

"My name is Sunami," he responded with admiration in his voice. "What's yours?"

She casually parted her legs and slowly caressed her thighs as if they were the only two people in the room.

"It should be Salami, Cuz you packing some meat in them jeans," she said.

"Her name is Everlyn," Outlaw began, "and she straight freak-a-leek, son. She like it any way you can handle it. And the pussy is outta this world, kid," he continued.

"See shorty right there," he said, pointing. "That's Vanessa, from Peekskill. She wants to be a porn star. And she got the bomb ass pussy between her legs," he expressed with conviction in his voice.

Sunami looked the Spanish woman over. She had blue eyes, long black hair, and thick, heart-shaped lips. Her body was curvaceous, and from the look of her face, she couldn't have been more than nineteen years old.

Two blunts and four drinks later, everyone deviated from their conversation. They began touching and caressing on the women like immature adolescents. Candy laid back on the sofa as others around her engaged in all-out sex.

Slowly, she spread her legs wide and slid a finger deep into her pussy. She closed her eyes and began rocking her hips back and forth while stroking her clit.

Shadow looked on at the orgy of bodies squirming on the sofa. "Let's go to the shower, Candy."

Heartbeats later, Candy and Shadow stood under streams of warm water flowing down on their naked bodies.

Hood Consigliere

They were entwined like cobras during mating season as they feverishly kissed one another. Candy pulled away from him. "Stand under the water for a minute. I wanna see what that meat looks like wet," she whispered.

Shadow was slightly taller than five feet nine with a muscular build. His skin was killer black, and he looked like greased-down leather as water washed down over his body.

"Aaahhh," he mumbled as she stroked his manhood back and forth with her hand. She eased in closer and licked his ear.

She knew he was from North Carolina and had plenty of money. Her dream was always to trap a man with money who could financially support her and take her out of the strip club. Alone with him in the shower, she began working her magic in all attempts to work a spell over him.

Suddenly, Shadow felt a chill throughout his body as Candy caressed him between his thighs, only inches away from his testicles. "Wait a minute," she said while adjusting the water to the coldest temperature possible. She reached for a citrus-scented body wash and started laughing as he yelled from the cold water assaulting his body.

What Shadow didn't know was that cold water would shrink his nuts and increase the power and pleasure of his orgasm. She gently rubbed his body with the liquid soap. She leaned her body against his and trailed her finger down his back until it reached the crack of his ass. He grabbed her wrist, holding her back.

He then stuck his finger into her, becoming more excited by her juice. He pulled out his finger and stuck it into her mouth. Hungrily, she sucked on it. She then kneeled down and gently sucked on his huge erection. Her lips roamed the length of his shaft with such skill. "Oh shit!" he yelled as his legs started to stiffen.

"Not yet, playboy," she said. Candy managed to balance herself on one leg as she placed the other one on the ledge of the tub, turning her hips upward. She spread her pussy lips with two fingers to allow him easy entry.

Surprisingly, he dropped to his knees and licked her clit with a very skilled tongue. The sensation overwhelmed her. She closed her eyes and yelled while holding his head, as his tongue flicked her highly sensitive spot.

Suddenly, he stopped and stood to his feet. She opened her eyes, looking as if she had lost all touch with reality. He stepped forward in between her thighs. He slid his dick slowly into her inner walls of velvet, inch by inch.

She gasped, feeling pain and pleasure as it hurt so good. She gave back to him by meeting his thrusts. She tensed and squeezed, as if she was trying to milk him dry.

His grasp tightened around her hips. She wrapped her arms around his neck to hold on for dear life. She began trembling.

"Oh fuck!" she yelled. "Oh god, I'm about to cum!"

In the distance, someone yelled, "Candy, you aight in there girl?" The voice was now on the other side of the bathroom door. "Sounds like he's killing you, girl. Outlaw wanna know if you going to the strip club with us?"

"Yess, yes, yes!" she responded while gasping for breath. "Ooohh, ooowww!"

"Oh god, yeah, I'm coming."

"Alright." Everlyn walked away from the door smiling.

Chapter 5

Cuba's restaurant was situated on the south side of Durham, the heart of the city's middle and upper-class business community. His restaurant was large, plush, and had the city's most elegant dance floor. Patrons spent lots of money at his club, and many gangsters met there to conduct illegal business.

The wall behind the bar was completely covered in mirrors, and overhead lights cast a soft glow throughout. A tall, slender, and beautiful woman with a girlish chest mixed drinks for all the customers. She looked toward the door and noticed two men enter the restaurant.

A beautiful, thick-hipped waitress with long hair was startled when the men passed by her quickly. Both men were well groomed and stood about the same height. One of the guys was dressed in a white hoody with black and white designs embroidered on the sleeves and around the neck.

The other man was wearing a black hoody and a platinum-encrusted diamond on his neck. They scanned all the faces as if they were looking for someone in particular. The waitress threaded her way around the tables to them. "Can I help you?" she asked, with a look of disapproval toward them.

"That depends on you, beautiful!"

"I meant, may I get you a table, sir?"

"No. My name is Omega. I'm here to see Mr. Sanchez. We have business to discuss. So, if you would please be so kind to inform him that I'm here, I'd appreciate it!"

She asked both men for ID because she found it hard to believe that these men were associates of Mr. Sanchez. Omega felt totally disrespected and decided to unzip his pants, and pulled out his long black penis.

Everyone who saw this uncouth spectacle gasped in disbelief. The waitress was speechless and now highly upset.

"Now, as you can see, I'm old enough to drink, fuck, and eat. Can you please do as I've instructed you?" Omega said with a stone-cold, hard look.

"I'm sorry, sir," said the waitress, with eyes studying his manhood much too long.

Omega looked around the restaurant and saw Mr. Sanchez sitting at a table far in the back with two other gentlemen. He walked in that direction while zipping his pants, and thanked the startled waitress with kindness in his voice.

He took one step and informed his partner, "E-Jay! Keep your eyes open, remain focused and on point," he said in a near whisper over his shoulder. "I'm not sure what this motherfucker wants from me."

Mr. Sanchez stood to his feet as the two thugs approached him. "How are you? Omega, E-Jay, glad you could make it." Mr. Sanchez shook both men's hands.

"Have a seat, make yourself comfortable." Omega took a seat at the table and E-Jay remained standing to his right, like a soldier on post.

Mr. Sanchez introduced Omega and E-Jay to the other two men at the table. "This is my brother, Mario. And this here is Mellow. He works for me."

"Good evening to you both," Omega said, "but why are we meeting here? Couldn't we have met somewhere else?"

"What? Are you kidding me? This is the best place in town. And besides, the food is wonderful here," Mr. Sanchez said as the startled waitress approached the table.

"Can I get you gentlemen anything?"

"Yes, bring us some drinks. What will you be having, Omega? Anything you want, it's on me."

"Thanks. I'll have a Green Hornet on the rocks."

"Mario, Mellow, and I will have our usual drinks, Ms. Sandria," said Cuba Sanchez as he leaned back in his chair.

Once the waitress was out of earshot, Cuba leaned in and folded his hands on the table. "Omega, my name is Mr. Sanchez. However, I prefer you call me Cuba. Indirectly, you and I have conducted business on more than one occasion by way of a middle man."

Omega looked at Cuba with question marks hidden in his eyes, wondering what was up with this clown. He had no idea what the hell he was talking about and was curious.

"Would you care to inform me of just what it is you're talking about?" Omega asked.

"Fair enough. But let me humor you a bit before getting down to business. See, it's like this. Whenever I have problems with your people, you've always handled them for me by way of a middleman who gave you names and cash for your services. I was the one financing those hits, and a lot of the time you had no idea you were working for me. Which brings us to this meeting."

The waitress appeared with their drinks. "Can I get you anything else, sir?"

"No, thank you. That will be all, Ms. Sandria," Cuba replied.

Once she walked off, Cuba reached inside his cashmere overcoat and removed a platinum case. He opened it and took out a Cuban cigar, lit it, and placed the case on the table.

"Now, as I was saying, because of your expertise, I want to now make you a team member and a generous offer. I'm offering you $75,000 a month whether you kill or not. You'll have the best lawyers money can buy. All expenses are on me. That's including your family also."

"Why me?" Omega asked, knowing there was a catch, and he didn't enjoy being the one caught, especially in a trap. Omega wanted an answer because he felt that something wasn't on the up and up.

"Like I stated earlier, we both have common interests and business together."

"And what would that be?" Omega inquired. Cuba looked into his eyes a second or two before speaking.

"When we have a problem with someone, we confront them and the problem face to face. Correct me if I'm wrong. See, right now I have a problem, and I need your help to solve that problem."

"So, you have a problem that you want me to confront for you?" Omega asked, sipping his drink.

"Yes and no. Basically, I'll confront the problem, but I need you to bring the problem to me. See, there's this guy who works for me, and while conducting business he was robbed of my money. And that creates the problem. No one takes from Cuba and lives."

Their eyes met for a short moment as Cuba pulled on the cigar. Omega was puzzled and didn't know exactly how to respond. Most niggas selling drugs in the Bull City sold for Cuba, but now Omega was being asked to become part of his family. *Too easy*, he thought.

"Okay, tell me more," Omega stated in a tone of voice that showed interest in Cuba's proposition.

"You see this fella here?" Cuba pointed to Mellow.

"This is the guy that got taken for my money. I will let him explain what happened and we'll go from there." Cuba smashed his cigar in the ashtray.

For fifteen minutes, Mellow explained the event in detail. However, he purposely failed to mention that his girlfriend and her sister were present. Mellow had no idea how dangerous a man Omega really was and how much he actually loved to kill, steal, and destroy people's lives. It was more than a thrill to him. It was all he knew how to accomplish without failing,

Omega had no belief in God, the law, politics, or anything else for that matter. He only believed in money, power, and assassinating key figures in the game. He lived by chance, life, and death. He was responsible for many of the unsolved deaths in the city over the past two years. Omega trusted no one other than his partner, E-Jay. They grew up together and were somewhat forced to survive by any means they found necessary.

The men ordered another round of drinks. When the waitress disappeared, Omega sipped from his glass and scanned the room out of habit. He noticed an older couple dining and drinking wine. The woman appeared to be around fifty years old. Despite her age, he found her very attractive and wondered what fucking her felt like.

"Has anyone attempted to find Sunami and Shadow?" Omega asked while lighting a Newport.

Mario, who was silent during the entire meeting, placed his glass on the table and said, "I've been searching for those scumbags all day. No one has seen them. Either that, or people don't want to tell me where they are."

Omega looked him over with scrutiny. Mario was large with dark eyes, a ruffled beard, and a larger than normal nose. "So now you want me to search the streets for them?" Omega asked coldly.

"Can you handle the job and bring them to me in one piece?" Cuba asked. "You see, if he's dead, then that means I can't reclaim and retrieve my money. This guy and his Shadow need to be made examples of right away. Otherwise, people all over town will be under the impression that I've gone soft, and I'm not having that," Cuba expressed angrily.

"You sound like a wounded animal seeking revenge," Omega said.

"Wounded? Ha, ha, ha. No! Disrespected, yes!" Cuba responded.

"In these streets, there's people who plot twist shit. Double crossers and thieves," Omega said in a serious tone.

Mario gazed into Mellow's eyes with the intensity of a laser beam. "Honor should be the number one principle in every man's life."

"So, you think I robbed Cuba, huh?" Mellow asked, feeling somewhat disrespected. "I know you not trying to play me short nigga, Cuz if you are, I'll—"

Omega interrupted, "Let me stop you before you dig your own grave too. I thought the same thing you thinking, and I'd be lying if I said the thought didn't cross my mind. You gotta look at every aspect and possibility. No need to be jumping to conclusions."

"I think this Sunami stalked the house out," Cuba speculated. "See, it's like he knew the best time to hit it. And my brother and I have known Mellow for a very long time. We know he don't go popping off at the gums like most. He's honest and solid."

"They don't make them like him anymore," Mario said while patting Mellow on the back in support of his brother's remark.

Omega thought about all the facts but wasn't inclined to believe everything he heard. "To me, it sounds as though they followed Mellow for weeks until they figured out his pattern and spotted his weaknesses before striking an attack."

"Now you're talking. I figured the same thing. That's why we got to hit this fucker back," Cuba expressed as a couple walked by them and toward the bar. "Now we have to send a message that they understand, because I don't want them thinking they can hit Cuba and not face me in the end."

"I agree with you. The consequences for ripping you off should be very severe," Omega said. "Deal me in the game. How will I be paid?"

Cuba was elated by Omega's decision to join the family. However, he knew that he would have to kill him and E-Jay after the job was finished. "Paying you is no problem." He reached into his overcoat and pulled out a thick, sealed, large envelope and tossed it on the table.

"Inside you'll find $75,000 in large bills. I know you can handle the situation," Cuba said, then sipped from his glass.

"Any questions? Feel free to ask."

"Yeah, this Sunami guy, I know him. Went to school with him years ago." Omega continued flipping through the bills as if he was checking a deck of cards.

"They shouldn't be that difficult to locate. Right now, they might be out of town. I'll find them for you…boss."

Cuba smiled. "Now we're in business. It's all there, no need to count it. When the job is done, there will be another $75,000 for you."

"Well, consider it done," Omega responded and stood to his feet. "Thanks for the drinks. I'll call you Monday night with details. I noticed the number you provided in the envelope."

"You're a wise man, Omega," Cuba said, shaking his hand. Omega finished his drink, left the restaurant with E-Jay, and walked three blocks down the street. Neither man spoke until they got into the car.

"So, what do you think?" E-Jay asked while searching through CDs. "You think he's on the up and up or what?"

"Nah, I don't trust him. Once the job is over, he's gonna try to off us," said Omega as he started the car and pulled off into the traffic.

"What makes you say that?" E-Jay asked, sounding slightly confused.

"A man that powerful don't leave loose ends untied. All those hit men he has working for him, why use us?"

"I don't know," said E-Jay. "He probably heard through the streets that we're good and know how to handle our business."

"That's my point. The only people who know about us is dead. We never left anyone alive. Here, count half out and keep it," Omega said as he tossed the envelope across the seat to E-Jay. "We'll do the job, collect that other $75,000, then we'll do one last job and relocate."

"What last job?" E-Jay asked while loading CDs.

"Killing Cuba, Mario, and Mellow. We ain't been leaving witnesses alive, so why the hell do you think we're gonna start now? They're not an exception to the rule. I'm not worrying about no Sunami either. If they want him, they can get him themselves. He's not my problem."

E-Jay reached down and turned down the volume.

"I thought we were gonna go after Sunami? So, if we're not gonna do it, you know there's gonna be some flack behind that shit. Then who we gonna get?"

Omega flashed a mischievous smile. "You'll see."

Omega already had a plan, and it was a surefire way to get over. Or at least he thought.

Keese

Chapter 6

The night sky twinkled with stars like diamonds. It was only seconds before midnight. The air was clear of its usual pollution and the atmosphere was crisp. The temperature had dropped slightly.

A large group of men and women gathered around the sidewalk outside of Fool's Paradise on Boston Road in the Bronx. People from all walks of life and various cities and states frequented this strip club.

Security guards wearing shirts two sizes too small were at the entry door. Cars of all sizes, colors, and makes crept along the street and stopped right by the red carpet of the VIP entrance door. Valet attendants opened the doors and escorted the guests inside as valet drivers got in the cars and drove them to a private parking lot.

Candy and Everlyn were inside the club, sitting at the bar. "So, do you think they're coming or not, girl? I mean, they said they were coming through," Candy asked.

"Well, they need to hurry up if they coming. I'm missing out on money," Everlyn said while reaching for her drink. She took a few sips and asked, "What do you think of Sunami?"

"What do you mean, what do I think of him? He aight, just quiet as hell," Candy replied while adoring herself in the overhead mirror.

"Girl, I tried everything. He didn't even want this pussy. Had his shit hard as hell and still wouldn't let me ride that dick."

"Maybe you just not his type."

"Oh, and you are?'

"Shit, a nigga always wants some white pussy, especially if it's Candy."

"Huh, I know some who won't even consider the thought of fucking you, so don't flatter yourself, sweetness!"

There was a moment of laughter between them.

"Girl, you ain't nothing but a freak."

"And a damn good freak too. And you just as freaky as me, so don't even try it, bitch," Everlyn laughed and stated seriously. "But in reality, you'll never really be fully accepted, so live with it, Candy Girl. What time you got?"

Candy checked her watch and wondered why the men hadn't shown up yet. "Girl, it's something after one, and them niggas still not here." The girls were ready to change and start working. But before they did, they went outside one last time to look for Outlaw, Sunami, and Shadow.

Candy and Everlyn went outside through the VIP entrance. "Girl, you ready to shake whatcha mama gave ya?" Everlyn asked, looking at the crowd in awe. "This motherfucker gonna be packed like crazy tonight. Seduction is supposed to be here tonight too. Did Seduction show up yet?" Everlyn asked the valet attendant.

"Yeah, she's been here since, ah, about twelve," he responded. "You received a message tonight." Candy looked surprised at the valet attendant. She never received calls during work hours. "Some guy named Shadow called. Said he'll be running a little late, and for you to wait up outside for him and his friends."

Both women spun around abruptly when they heard loud music off in the distance, which got louder by the second. They scanned up and down the street. *Aight, new drink, one part Alize, one part Cristal, Thug Passion, baby...* Tupac's voice screamed over Outlaw's beats... *Y'all know what time it is. This drink is guaranteed to get the pussy wet and the dick hard. Now if ya with me, pour a glass and drink with a nigga. Know what I mean?*

Both women saw the two cars approaching as the music became even louder. *I ain't trying to turn y'all niggas into alcoholics, I'm trying to turn you into motherfucking thugs. So come and get some of this Thug Passion, baby.*

"Girl, look at this fool. He the craziest nigga I ever seen," Everlyn said, pointing toward the street. Outlaw was hanging out of the passenger window of his CL 500 Mercedes Benz coupe as Sunami pulled over to the curb.

Shadow stopped behind him in the white Ferrari.

An attractive female with black hair and sparkling eyes approached Shadow and said, "Damn, nigga, you fine as hell. I love to drive a stick. What you say we get outta here together?" She was suddenly pushed violently with such force that she stumbled sideways before regaining her balance. "Bitch, you need to watch where you going before I kick your white ass outta here!" she grumbled.

Candy quickly reached into her purse and pulled out a push-button switch blade. "No, you the bitch, and what you need to do is get out of my face before you get fucked out here and lose that pretty face, ho! Now go find yourself another playground to play in, bitch!"

The girl looked Candy up and down. She refused to back down. Candy decided to make her move. She raised her hand back to strike the girl across the face, when suddenly her arm was caught by Outlaw. "Candy, put that shit up!"

"Everything ok?" asked a security guard.

"Yeah, she cool. Just a misunderstanding, that's all," said Outlaw.

"Misunderstanding my ass!" the woman yelled over Outlaw's shoulder.

"That bitch was about to get her white ass kicked, coming up to me with that rah-rah bullshit!" she continued as Candy walked off.

Outlaw glanced over his shoulder. He took a second to capture a picture of the woman in his mind. "Yo, if shorty comes anywhere near you, I'ma bust that bitch ass," Outlaw swore to Candy.

"Candy, listen, me and my niggas need your help on something before we go inside."

"What?" she asked with a quick glance sideways.

"Y'all, what? You know I'm against doing that crazy ass shit," she said, meeting his eyes with a stare.

"I tried to tell Shadow, but..."

"Oh, Shadow told you to ask me, huh?" she interrupted.

"No, I asked you cause we don't take no damn chances when we around these type motherfuckers."

"Baby girl, listen," Shadow said while approaching her, "he's right. I didn't know how you would respond. My burner is like a Mastercard, I never leave home without it. And you asked me to come here with you because you had something to show me. So, look out for me, ma. Just this one time."

She looked into his eyes and took a deep breath. *He is so cute,* she thought to herself, knowing she would do anything to please him. "Okay, I'll carry two of them in, but Everlyn is gonna have to carry Outlaw's."

They walked rapidly across the street to a secluded area behind a brick building. Candy took the chrome 45's from Shadow and Sunami, and Everlyn took Outlaw's 9mm Glock. Candy concealed one in the front waistline of her panties and stashed the second one in the back. Everlyn nervously did the same.

They all walked back toward the club in silence.

Sunami wondered how he would handle the situation if the girls were caught with the guns. Getting caught didn't bother him half as much as not having a backup plan for his next move.

Two bouncers stopped them as they approached the VIP entrance. "Hi, Nick," Everlyn said to the tall older one.

"When you gonna come inside for a lap dance?" she asked in a soft, sexy, and distracting voice.

"Now you know that's against policy, but since it's you asking, I'll think about it."

Everlyn and then Candy stepped quickly through the metal detector, and it went off. "Candy, you got a gun on you?" the bouncer asked playfully.

"Yeah, matter of fact, I got two big 45's on me, daddy. I like 'em big."

"I bet you do," he said and laughed.

"Nah, I got metal wire in my bra. You wanna see?" she said as she squeezed her 44 double Ds together.

"Get your crazy ass in there before you poke somebody's eyes out with those things."

"Thanks," she said, happy that she was in the clear. "These gentlemen are with us tonight, so give them VIP passes, okay!"

"No problem. Here you go, fellas, have a nice night and enjoy yourselves," Nick said as he handed them the passes. As they entered the club, there was a large poster hanging on the wall to the right of a gorgeous feature entertainer named Seduction. Sunami was mesmerized by the beauty of the woman on the wall. He had the feeling he'd seen this woman somewhere before but couldn't remember where.

"Yo, Shadow, didn't we see this woman dance at the Foxy Lady Club in Raleigh?"

Shadow studied the poster for a few seconds. "I don't really know, son, but shorty is a dime for real. Man, look at that body!"

Outlaw read the text on the poster out loud, "Tonight see and meet the top supermodel and diva. Seduction will be dancing for all your wannabe players and ballers. So, you think you got game, think you got long money, then test your skills with Seduction and enter Fool's Paradise."

"She not giving shit up. She comes out, get a nigga dick hard as a brick, and bounce on your ass," Outlaw warned Sunami.

"Nigga, that's Cuz you slacking in the macking," he said. "I got's to holla. I'm telling you, I seen her some place before."

"Yeah, in your dreams last night, nigga." Shadow and Outlaw laughed.

As they went from the lobby into the main club, their eyes had to adjust to the black lights and flashing red and blue strobe lights. There was a long waistline-high stage in the center of the floor. Players sat around the stage hypnotized by a tall, curvaceous, and pretty light-skinned young woman. Her ass bounced to the beat of "Shake Ya Ass" by Mystical.

Ballers, gangsters, pimps, macks, hustlers, drug pushers, rappers, lesbians, and thieves tossed money in different denominations at her feet.

Candy and Everlyn were the next dancers up and performed a girl on-girl show. They drove the crowd wild, and the men threw so much money at the stage. By the time they finished, the girls had two large piles of cash.

"Man, it smells like straight pussy in this mother," yelled Outlaw.

"Everlyn and Candy did their thing, for real, kid."

"I know I tossed about a 'G' up there," said Shadow. "Can't wait to get that back at the crib. That trick suck dick really good."

"Do she?" Sunami asked.

"Do she! That bitch suck dick like a postage stamp licking machine."

Suddenly, spinning multicolored lights brought the stage back to life, and a fog machine sent a thick white cloud across the stage and through the club. Soon the stage was covered in a cloud. A pair of red stilettos appeared from nowhere, and then a curvaceous 45-28-45 body built for sin strutted down the long stage. Jet-black hair cascaded down in her face and covered all but her voluptuous lips.

Seduction lived up to her stage name, as she danced to "Seems Like You Ready" by R. Kelly. As she turned toward Sunami, their eyes locked. "Oh shit!" he yelled out.

A slight smile came across her face as she walked like a panther over to where he was seated. She turned her back to him and slowly got down on all fours and gyrated her big ass in front of his face. She looked back with a quick glance at Sunami. She came down off the stage, stood in front of him, dropped her hair into his lap, and slowly ran her fingers up his thighs. She stood up and removed her bra, caressed her enormous breasts, and pinched her nipples.

Sunami was intoxicated by her soft skin and sweet fragrance. She sat on his lap, and their eyes were locked. She found him devilishly attractive. She sensed instantly that he was more dangerous than any man she'd ever known. He gripped her waist with one hand as she gyrated slowly on him. He was overpowered by her soft, warm flesh. She slipped both of her hands around his neck. She positioned herself so that she could move her hips back and forth and stroke his dick with her moist pussy through the thin fabric of her thong.

As the song came to an end, she stood up slowly and they continued to look into each other's eyes without saying a word. He stuck two $100 bills into the back of her thong. "Thank you," Seduction said as she leaned down to kiss Sunami on the cheek.

"Baby, you could sit on my face and let me guess your weight." Seduction smiled at him, then turned and walked away slowly.

He reached out and caressed her ass cheek as she walked off. She looked back at him and flashed a sexy smile.

"Nigga, you got to be the luckiest man alive," Outlaw said.

Sunami looked like he'd just awakened from a dream when he stood to his feet and walked off in search of Seduction.

"Yo, where you going?" Shadow asked.

"To get that phone number I threw away today."

Seduction entered her dressing room and closed the door behind her. "Damn, what the hell was I thinking out there?" She was startled by a knock at the door. "Be out in a minute."

"May I speak with you a sec?" implied the voice on the other side of the door. "Are you always dry humping a man, just to leave him in pain?"

"How did you get past security?"

"You'd be surprised what I can do. But you still haven't answered my question."

She was about to speak, but suddenly realized that she didn't owe him any kind of explanations. "Get in here before someone sees you." She stepped back from the door, allowing him to enter.

"I just came by to ask if you would join me later for a drink?"

She tried hard to pretend that she wasn't mesmerized by his voice and country grammar. "That'll be nice. Can you give me a few minutes to freshen up?"

"Aight, I'll be at the bar in the VIP section."

*

Chapter 7

Muted voices floated from the VIP tables while sounds of clinking glasses rang out. Sunami looked around for his entourage. He saw them seated in a circular booth by the bar and made his way through the crowd toward them.

"What up, people? I see y'all started without me, huh?" he said as he slid into the booth. "She'll be out here in a few. Now you tell me who's slacking in their macking?"

"Nigga, you running game. You know damn well you didn't holla at no Seduction. How the hell you game a stunt like that, son?" Outlaw asked.

"My nigga, I slid into the restroom across the hall from the security and valet. I found one of those valet jackets, put it on, and crept past their asses to the back, smooth at Carlito so I could do the damn thang. Just like in the movie, son. Once I got back there, I threw the shit in the trash and knocked on her door. Straight gangsta, nigga," he said, locking eyes with Outlaw as if they were still little kids.

Outlaw read the look in his eyes, knowing that look all too well. "Man, what the fuck is the A&P shit!"

"That's what I used to do back in the day. I'd go into A&P and find me one of those vest or aprons, put that shit on. I'd hit the back, open, and take shit home."

They all burst out laughing.

"What y'all laughing at? Shit, I wanna laugh too," said Everlyn as she approached the table.

"You know thugs don't get drunk, we get crunk, little mama!" Shadow responded. Candy and Everlyn slid into the booth.

"What y'all up to?" Candy asked.

"Not much, shorty. Just enjoying the night, that's all. Why? What's up with you?" Shadow asked her.

"Not a damn thang! Just can't wait to get home. These heels killing my feet."

"I can't wait to get you outta them heels."

"Shut up, nasty. You ain't getting any. I'm going home and going to bed. You have no idea how fucking tired I am right now."

"That's why a little time on your back tonight is what you need."

"You the most sexually aroused nigga I ever met."

Shadow took a sip of his drink and sat it back down on the table. "You weren't complaining in the shower when I freaked your ass."

"No, you didn't! I'm the one that freaked you. You know my candy was damn good. That's why your ass begging now."

"Man, you two are off the chain for real," Sunami said and stood to his feet. "I'ma go get some drinks."

"Nah, son. I got you. Just parlay," said Outlaw. "I need to peep something anyway, feel me?"

"Do you, nigga."

Shadow had a plan to get back at Candy and suddenly spoke up. "Bring me a Thug Passion and Candy a Hennessey Red."

Outlaw and Sunami laughed because they knew Hennessey mixed with Red Bull was like liquid Viagra.

"Girl, you better not drink that mess," said Everlyn.

"You'll be fucking like you're fueled by nitroglycerin. Your ass will be begging him to hit that shit sixty-nine different ways."

"How the hell do you know?" Candy asked.

"Girl, don't even play me. I heard about it from someone."

After everyone ordered, Outlaw walked off to the bar. When he got back to the booth with a tray full of drinks, a smile of victory covered his face.

"Damn, yo, what took you so long?" Sunami asked.

"Shorty at the bar, she wanted to peep game. So, I spit at her a little something and got her number. Just checking if I was slacking on my macking, but it's still tight, son."

Abruptly, everyone's attention turned to Seduction as she approached the booth. "Hope I'm not interrupting you all."

Sunami gazed into her eyes, searching. He stood to his feet and made room for her in the booth. "You look stunning."

She slid into the booth. Sunami took a seat next to her. The tantalizing scent of her perfume filled his nostrils.

"Your perfume smells good. What is it?"

"It's called soap and water. You smell good yourself. What are you wearing?"

"Eternity."

"Uhm hmm. Are you going to introduce us to shorty or what?" Outlaw said.

Everlyn quickly kicked Outlaw under the table.

"You know her name, why you tripping?"

"What's up, Seduction?" Outlaw asked, laughing.

"Why you not getting that money tonight?"

Refusing to explain herself to him, she looked over to Everlyn. "How you, Eve, Candy? So, you know Sunami, I take it."

"Yeah, we met them today at Outlaw's," Everlyn replied.

Seduction reached under the table and lightly tapped Sunami on his leg. "Some guy is on his way to this table. He probably trying to take me to bed or something."

"You want me to handle scrams?" Outlaw asked.

"Nah, let him approach. I'll be okay." When he arrived at their table, she asked, "May I help you, player?"

"Yeah, can I get a lap dance tonight like you gave him?"

"I don't know about that. No hard feelings."

"Shit, why wouldn't you? A nigga like me can do things for you."

Seduction crossed her arms over her chest. "Oh, you got it like that, I suppose?"

"I'm saying, shorty, we can do this lap dance thing, then afterward we can get a few drinks."

"I have that already!"

"Then we can get a room," he continued, disregarding her sarcasm.

"I have my own condo," she replied.

Sunami laughed at the scene and said, "How 'bout this. Let me drive you home in my Ferrari." He paused and glanced at the guy, then into Seduction's eyes. "We can go to your house and continue what we started. We can get better acquainted, and in the morning, I can cook breakfast for you and serve it in bed."

"Can you be more specific with getting acquainted?" she said, leaning back while staring at Sunami.

"Oh, so you want details, huh? First, I'll slowly undress you, and we'll take a long hot shower. Then, we'll enter the chamber of Seduction," he continued, as if there was no one around to hear the conversation.

The way he spoke made her feel a warmness she couldn't explain. "You had me at breakfast in bed."

"Sorry, Doc," Sunami said to the man. "I guess you'll be masturbating tonight, player. No Seduction in your life, now burn up the road, duke." Everyone in the booth burst out laughing as the guy walked off with a defeated look on his face.

"I didn't think you was gonna keep a straight face."

"I'm not all that good with expressing myself," Sunami confessed.

"Yeah, you got to give credit where credit is due. He was nice with it."

"Yo, you see scram's grill?" Shadow cut in. "When he smiled, he looked like a fucking crocodile with Buckwheat eyes." Everlyn nearly spit her drink out.

"Man, did you see the look on his face?" asked Outlaw. "Yo, word on my mother, dude looked like he was hit with a bag full of Stephen King horror books."

Once the laughter ceased, Seduction turned to face Sunami. "Did you mean it when you said you'd cook for me?"

"Hypnotic, I meant every word I said, because where I'm from, we keep shit real with our women, and expect the same kind of respect from them also."

Suddenly three guys and a female were heading their way.

Shadow noticed that one of them was the man Seduction turned down. "Sunami, look, coming this way."

"They got that bitch. I was about to fuck up with them too," Candy cut in.

"Yo, country boy! Let's step outside fo' a minute. And bring that white bitch with you too! My sister says she pulled a knife on her."

All three men quickly stood up, pushed by their survival instincts. Seduction looked on. "Don't fight them, Sunami. It's...they're not worth it. It serves no purpose!"

"What you think about it, Outlaw?" Sunami asked, wanting a second opinion.

"Umm...they all look like pussy waiting to be fucked."

"Bitch, I'ma slap the taste of last night's dick out your mouth!" Candy yelled to her adversary.

"I'm with you, Candy," Everlyn added, rising to her feet.

Unexpectedly, Seduction stood up and left the booth. "You have my number, call me, and please don't lose it this time." She walked off and disappeared into the thick of the crowd.

"So, what's up, you niggas want it or what?" asked one of the guys.

"Punk motherfucker, we 'bout to show you heaven ain't hard to find," Outlaw yelled back.

"Cool, we be seeing you motherfuckers soon," the other guy said while backing away.

Outlaw and his friends were heated and felt disrespected by being called out. They all sat and came up with a plan to demolish the situation and gain what they felt they deserved.

"Picture me scared of a motherfucker that eat, shit, sleep, and bleed like me. Trust me, I'm killing all them motherfuckers on sight," Outlaw told Sunami.

"They'll be out there somewhere when we bounce," Shadow cut in.

"I doubt it. Too many security guards will be around," Everlyn said.

"She right, people always go over there behind McDonald's because the highway is right there," Candy added.

"You think them niggas got heat?" Shadow asked, refusing to underestimate a foe.

"Don't matter, we going head on like a fucking army, cause I'm blazing out the gate. Ain't got no damn words," said Sunami. "Cool, shits closing now, let's bounce."

Once outside, the valets parked their cars and passed them keys. Sunami and Shadow rode together, while Candy, Everlyn, and Outlaw followed them closely from behind.

Their plan was to remain five car lengths apart, since no one knew what the enemy was driving or how the attack would come. They had been driving around the Bronx for twenty minutes or so, nervously talking with one another and ready for whatever.

"We might as well go home. The cowards ain't nowhere to be found," Everlyn suggested. Outlaw checked his rearview mirror and noticed a silver Navigator speeding down the hill toward them.

A rush of adrenaline kicked through his body. He floored the accelerator and steered toward the open outside lane.

"Everlyn! Call Sunami and tell him to drop back quick. Them niggas is on our ass."

"Where?" She looked around wildly as she pressed the numbers on her cell phone.

"Directly behind us, the Navigator. I know it's them." He reached for the 9mm Glock he put between the seats.

Everlyn handed the phone to Candy when Sunami answered. Shadow frantically searched the street for others that may be with them. He saw no other vehicles.

"What the fuck is that, a cannon?" Candy asked.

"It's my baby. An F.N. 9mm with a thirteen-round clip full of heart-stopping hollow points," Outlaw spat as he checked his side mirrors. "You ever shot a Calico?"

"A what?" she asked wildly. The Navigator was closing in at high speed.

"A fucking Calico!" He looked around to check on Everlyn in the back seat. "You good back there?"

"Yes."

"Candy, look under the seat and get that burner out," he said while hitting the button on his door. Candy's seat automatically slid back, and she bent to retrieve a 9mm Calico M950 from under the seat.

She looked in disbelief at the size of the gun. As she lifted it up, she couldn't believe how heavy it was. "God, what is this? You could kill a whole fucking army with this big ass shit."

"Look, when they get close, stick that bitch out the window and talk to them punk motherfuckers with it. And don't wait for no damn answers."

A sudden explosion of gunshots came from behind.

Outlaw checked the rearview mirror as both women screamed and ducked down.

More shots rang out, and the back windshield exploded into fragments, showering Everlyn in the back seat.

Shadow cut loose from Sunami's car. He pulled the trigger of a 40 caliber twice, missing the Navigator.

Outlaw slowed his car. The Navigator accelerated to his right and pulled up beside them. Outlaw immediately slammed on the brakes. The Navigator whizzed by, just as Candy leaned out the window and squeezed off four quick shots. A foot-long flame blazed from the barrel, and the driver's side window of the Navigator exploded.

The Navigator momentarily swerved in and out of lanes. Candy continued to shoot. Outlaw floored the gas pedal and pulled up behind their enemy. Sunami slowed his car and boxed the Navigator in. Shadow quickly dumped what was left in his clip into the cabin of the SUV.

All of a sudden, the Navigator swerved wildly and suddenly straightened out. Two gunmen leaned out both back windows and took aim as a third man leaned out the front passenger window. One of the backseat gunmen held a semi-automatic gun capable of shooting thirty rounds. He squeezed the trigger back.

Candy tried to duck back into the car when she saw the gunmen, but she reacted seconds too late. Her head snapped back and exploded into small chunks of meat, brain matter, and skull fragments.

"Candy! Candy!" Outlaw gripped her pants and pulled her body back into the car. Shadow emptied his clip into the windshield of the Navigator, which continued to move at high speed.

Shadow thumbed his clip release button and slammed another clip in place. He fired rapidly until the clip was empty. He saw the Navigator make a sharp left turn into a parking lot. "Shit, turn around, they trying to bounce!"

Sunami stood up on the brakes, quickly maneuvered a three-point turn, and headed toward the parking lot.

Outlaw followed. He was sure they were attempting to hit the other side, which let out onto another street.

When Outlaw looked over at Candy's lifeless body, he knew he had to kill them now. Do unto them as they did unto her. He blocked out Everlyn's screams, floored the gas, and the front of his Mercedes raised higher. He saw Sunami and Shadow behind him in the rearview mirror. The Navigator exited the parking lot and gunned through a red light crossing 241st.

Sunami fish tailed through the red light and crossed the intersection at about 70 mph. The Ferrari tires screeched in every gear he hit as he accelerated to 105 mph. "You ready to go Dirty South on these New York niggas?"

"Nigga, just pull up on them. I got this!" Shadow responded with vengeance in his eyes.

"Shoot them niggas tires out or something. We got to stop them before the cops see us. I ain't fucking going to jail!"

The Navigator turned quickly. Sunami down shifted and banked a hard left. Shadow gripped his pistol with two hands and fired. He realized he missed and fired off four more quick ones. The back end of the Navigator dropped down low.

The SUV swerved sideways in the road, jumped the curb, and crashed into a pizza shop.

Sirens could be heard in the distance, drawing closer with each passing second. Sunami drove like a bat out of hell. There was complete silence in both Sunami's and Outlaw's cars.

An hour later, they left Candy's body on the steps of a church. They couldn't bear just dumping her body anywhere. Shadow felt responsible for her death. He felt like he could have reacted faster to prevent it.

"Shadow, it's not your fault. Candy always lived her life on the edge," said Everlyn. "You did what you could. I'm the one who should have helped her, but I covered up like a little girl."

"You were just scared. Life goes on for all of us. It's either kill or be killed."

Everlyn knew that this night would forever change her outlook on life. She decided to move to North Carolina. There was nothing left for her in New York since she no longer had Candy at her side.

Keese

Chapter 8

Everlyn did most of the driving to North Carolina while Sunami and Shadow napped off and on along the way.

The Monday afternoon sun beamed through Sunami's bedroom curtains. He was motionless and sound asleep. The silence that filled the room was broken by the ringing of a phone.

Sunami rolled over and checked the caller ID. He recognized the number. "Hello."

"What's good, nigga? It's like two, and you still crashing, kid?" Outlaw laughed.

"Fuck you, nigga! I was tired as hell, man. What you up to?"

"Shit, just chillin'. What time did y'all get to the crib last night?"

"About ten something. Everlyn did most of the driving. When me and Shadow woke up, we were in fucking VA someplace. She got lost, but it's all good."

"How she feeling?"

"She taking it pretty good. A little hurt, but she good."

"Where she at now?"

"She in the living room, on the sofa, I think. Didn't want to go to bed. She stayed up late watching TV and drinking my shit."

There was a light moment of laughter between them.

"That sounds like her," Outlaw said. "You think she'll keep quiet?"

Sunami was silent for a moment. "No question!"

"Why you just get quiet like that?"

"Mmmm...yo, I think she running from something. I can't figure out why she just up and left like that. Got to be something more to it."

"Why you say that, son?"

"Because it just doesn't make sense to me, that's all."

"Maybe she just scared, thinking someone saw us and felt leaving was best."

"Maybe," Sunami replied.

"Yo, you remember that chick, Vanessa?"

"Yeah!"

"She called me a minute ago talking some crazy shit." Outlaw paused. "Bitch called here talking 'bout Candy was all on the news and said that the police called her when they found her phone number in her phone book."

Sunami was now wide awake and replaying the event in his mind.

He tried to think of any mistakes they might have made along the way. "Say word!"

"Word, son! Said they wanted to know who she was with last, or if Vanessa knew where she went the night before. I'm about to go see her now, soon as I get dressed and take my ride to this crackhead shop."

"You think she gonna talk about us too?" Sunami asked with worry in his voice.

"Nah, she not gonna talk. I got this one. Trust me?"

"Yeah, cousin. So do you think it's necessary?"

"No question! That's why that nigga Main is locked down now in Scotland. Can't be no other way."

Both men knew that if the police questioned Vanessa and she told them who Candy was with, they would become suspects in the investigation.

"Aight, do you, son. Just be careful, my nigga. Hit me back tonight when you straight, aight?"

"No question!"

"Keep checking on my ride for me and let me know when it's ready. I got to turn this rental car back in ASAP."

"Aight, holla back, son. You gonna holla at Seduction?"

"Yeah, I'ma call her as soon as I get up out of this bed. I want a baby with shorty."

"I feel ya! Man, let me bounce, you not about to keep me on the phone all day."

"I know that's right. We gonna holla," said Sunami.

"One!"

"Aight," Outlaw responded and hung up.

Hood Consigliere

As Sunami walked across the room, he couldn't stop thinking about how beautiful Hypnotic was. There was a knock at his bedroom door. "Yo," he yelled across the room.

Everlyn cracked the door and looked around. "It's me, may I come in?"

"Shit, you might as well, being you already in the room."

She stepped into the room. She was wearing black spandex shorts, a tight white t-shirt, and Nike running shoes.

She was actually looking pretty damn good to Sunami.

"I made you breakfast. I hope you don't mind that I took it upon myself to find my way around in your kitchen," she said with her eyes focused on the bulge in his boxers. "I know you hungry. You hardly ate anything yesterday."

"Can you cook? Or should I ask, what did you cook?"

Sunami smiled, knowing she had just made a pass at him.

She left the room and he took a shower and got dressed. He then went to the kitchen, where Everlyn and Shadow were conversing.

"Damn, girl, you cooked enough food to feed a prison cell block! The eggs look like they banging," said Sunami.

"Shorty got mad skills in the kitchen, Sunami. I haven't stopped eating since I sat down," Shadow said, raising a fork full of eggs to his mouth. "So, what we gonna do today?"

"I'm not quite sure yet," Sunami responded. "I'm gonna call Seduction and see if she'll fly down to spend some time with a brother. Whatcha think?"

"Shit, try! All she can say is no, but I think she'll come."

"What if she's afraid to fly?"

"She's not! Buy her some tulips and a box of chocolates... she'll definitely come," Everlyn said, smiling.

"How you know?" Sunami asked as he sliced through his pancakes.

"Because, us girls, we talk... I think you two look cute together."

"How much do you know about her?" Sunami asked.

"Her real name is Rashonda Hypnotic Smith, never been married, no kids, and she's very much available. She hasn't fucked anyone in six months. The only thing I can't tell you is her real age, but that doesn't matter anyway, does it?"

Sunami nearly choked on his eggs. "Damn, no wonder!" he said, then suddenly stopped speaking. *That explains her facial expression when she gave me that lap dance*, he thought to himself.

"How do you go from being a teacher to an exotic dancer?" he asked Everlyn.

"Teacher? She wasn't no damn teacher. She used to be—" Everlyn abruptly stopped talking. She realized she was about to reveal something he didn't know, a secret that Hypnotic didn't tell too many people. Everlyn wasn't comfortable telling him now.

"You gonna tell us or what? Was she a hooker or something?" he asked. "I'm saying, tell us."

"Nah, I don't get down like that, baby!"

"Down like what, I definitely ain't no fucking cop."

"I never thought you was, considering what happened Saturday night. I can't be airing her business. We cool, and I don't need to lose another friend. Call her, she's an honest kind of person. Tell her you can't stop thinking about her." Everlyn walked toward the sink to do the dishes.

"Yo, what the fuck was all that I'm not telling shit?" Sunami asked Shadow, looking somewhat confused.

"Man, you know how women are. They keep secrets between them. That's how my mom is too. Just ask her when you call her if you really need to know. I told you about stressing that crazy small shit! We just jacked a quarter of a mill' last week, and you stressing over some pussy. Man, we can have any hoe we want right now. Holla at shorty and see what's poppin'."

Sunami glanced at his diamond-encrusted watch. The time read 2:33. He decided it was the perfect time. He entered his bedroom, walked over to the phone, picked it up, and dialed Hypnotic's number.

He nervously sat down on the bed, anticipating what to say if she answered.

"Hello?"

"Ah...hello, may I speak to Hypnotic?"

"Speaking."

"How you doing, beautiful?"

"Oh, Sunami!"

"Yeah, who you think it was, baby?"

"I knew it was you, because no other man has my home phone number. But I am shocked that you called me."

"Yeah? Well, I was just sitting here thinking about you and all the wonderful things we could actually be doing together."

"That's so sweet. No one has ever told me that before."

"Well, that's because your destiny hasn't been set to cross my path yet. But now it's time for you to enjoy all the wonderful things in life you really deserve with the one who adores you for you."

"You kidding me, right?"

"No! I'm not playing no games. I take life seriously at all times, and I'm a good judge of character, too. Do you have anything up for today?"

"Well, that all depends," she responded playfully.

"On what?" he asked.

"Depends on what you have in mind."

"How 'bout you and I…ahh…"

"Oh! You and I, huh?"

"Yeah! You and I alone, how 'bout we go out to dinner? I know a nice Cuban restaurant with great cooks."

"So, you're asking me out?"

Refusing to answer, he continued to speak, "Once we're finished eating, we can catch a movie or just talk if you like. I know we've only spent a little time together, but I find myself very attracted to you. I'm already missing you. You touched a part of me that I can't control."

"Excuse me, what have I done?"

"I guess I'm asking you out on a date."

"Okay, I accept. Just let me make a few phone calls to cancel my appointments for today and tonight."

"For real?" He sounded surprised.

"Yeah, I'm for real. What time will you be picking me up?"

"I won't be picking you up."

"Huh?"

"You're going to use my credit card number, arrange a flight to RDU airport, and I'll pick you up there."

"I see you're very organized with your business affairs. I like that in a man."

"Yeah, I am, but this is not business, baby. It's the beginning of a beautiful friendship."

"Alright," she whispered in a low, sexy voice.

"You're something else. I'll book the flight and call you back with the arrival time, okay?"

"What will you be wearing?"

"You'll have to wait and see. Talk to you later. Bye."

Sunami was elated that things went well, and he looked forward to the day ahead. He couldn't wait to put down his game on his own turf.

After making his plans, Sunami briefed Shadow on their business affairs.

"Can you handle it?" he asked Shadow.

"No problem. What about that nigga, Nickel Bag? Don't he owe $125,000 for last week's drop off?"

"Oh yeah! Check that nigga, no shorts with him. So, if he doesn't have it, then you decide what's what. Take care of that."

"So, we looking at what from him?" Shadow asked.

"Double, $250,000. Anything over is his." Sunami placed his gun into the holster under his Armani suit jacket.

"I should be back around 9:00 p.m. I'll be here if you need me."

"What you want Everlyn doing while I do this?"

"Keep her close to you. Sometimes a second hand gives strength when needed. Strap her with a gun. If pushed, I know she'll bust now."

Shadow went down the hall to the living room to wait for Everlyn. He picked up a remote and turned on the radio. Moments later, Everlyn came into the living room.

"How do you like it?" she asked, spinning for him to admire. She wore a stunning white jacket and a skirt and some funky sandals that showed off her diamond-tipped pedicure.

Shadow was amazed. She was a dime and he looked forward to spending the day with her by his side. "Damn, Everlyn, what the fuck you trying to do? You want a nigga to have a heart attack or something?"

"Nigga, you just wanna get in my panties."

"Panties! Damn, I didn't think you had on any under there."

"Oh, so you were undressing me with your eyes?"

"I plead the fifth under the grounds I may incriminate myself."

"What we gonna do today?" she asked.

"Well, first, I have to conduct some business, see a few people and what not, but we're straight after that. What would you like to do?"

"Let's go out to eat, and then maybe catch a flick. You with it?"

"Are you asking me for a date?" he asked, catching her off guard.

"No! But we can act like we're on a date. I don't see no problem with that. Do you?"

Shadow sat down on the plush leather sofa, taking a moment to think before he responded. He lit a blunt and slowly inhaled. "Suppose I want to make love to you?"

She walked over and sat beside him. "I think if it's meant to happen, it will." She took the blunt from him and inhaled deeply.

"Come on, let's go handle some business before Sunami gets back."

"Give me a minute, I need to get my pocketbook."

When she returned, she followed Shadow to the garage. He opened the door and she saw two Hummers, a Benz, a Beamer, and two motorcycles.

"Y'all niggas getting it for real, huh?" She looked at the bikes and smiled.

"What you smiling at?"

"Just thinking about the time Candy taught me how to ride one of those."

"You know how to ride a bike"

"What? Do I know how to ride a bike? I might ride better than you!"

"Are you calling me out or something?"

"Take it any way you want, but I ride hard."

"So, you ride hard, huh?"

"I ride better than anyone you've ever known. So, what ride you gonna drive?" she asked, changing the subject.

"Let's ride this," he said, pointing toward the large black Hundeville. The headlights, front grille, and hood had all been modified and transformed into a Cadillac Escalade spec.

They climbed inside, then he started the engine and pressed a button on the console that opened the garage door.

"I love this song right here," she said as Maxwell filled her ears with soothing words of love.

"On the real, when I first saw you, I wondered what it would be like to make love to you," said Shadow.

"Umm... you did?"

"I hope you feel me the same way I'm feeling you, cause I'm being real."

"I'm feeling you! There's no doubt about that, Shadow."

His phone rang. "Hello."

"What's up. You alright?" Sunami asked.

"Yeah, I'm cool. Where you at?"

"I'm about twenty minutes away from my future wife. I can't believe I'm nervous."

"You'll be alright. Just be you, and no games. Keep shit the way you do."

"No doubt. You hit any spots yet?"

"I'm on the way now. I figure I'll hit Jackson Street first. What you think?"

"Whatever, son, you know the game and what you're doing. Just be careful."

"Aight."

"Where Everlyn at?"

"Right here beside me."

"What y'all got planned for tonight, gangster?"

"Nothing really."

"I bet you don't. Play on, nigga. I'll talk to you later."

Hood Consigliere

When Shadow got off the phone, Everlyn leaned across the seat and kissed him. "What was that for?"

"That was because I like you, on the real," she said softly.

He didn't know how to respond. He was now convinced that he had her right where he wanted her. "You ever shot a gun?"

There was a moment of silence between them.

"Yes," she finally answered. "Why?"

"If I hold you down, will you hold me down?"

"Yeah, if I have to," she replied.

More than anything, he wanted to know if she would kill when confronted with a threat head on. He wanted her ready for the unexpected.

"Look under the seat. There's a .380 there for you. Put it in your purse, and if you have to use it, don't even think twice. Okay?"

She placed it in her purse, closed her eyes, and leaned back in the seat.

Keese

Chapter 9

Sunami arrived at the airport and parked alongside the curb by the main entrance to the terminal. He glanced impatiently at his watch. It was 5:04. Her plane should have arrived already.

He reached over to the passenger seat and picked up the tulips, box of chocolates, and a Hallmark card.

People of many different nationalities scrambled through the main doors toward awaiting cabs and limos, while a few looked around for loved ones or a familiar car to pick them up.

Sunami carefully scanned the crowd for Hypnotic.

He did not want to miss her, since she had no idea what he was driving. As Hypnotic walked toward the door, she felt slightly nervous when she spotted Sunami. They looked directly into each other's eyes. She had no clue exactly how she would greet him.

She felt like a high school girl on prom night. She wondered whether or not she was dressed appropriately, did her hair look fine, etc., etc.

"Excuse me," she said after bumping into an older man. "I'm sorry, sir."

"No apology required, young lady," the man said, eyeing her with lust behind his smile.

She then walked through the double door and walked toward Sunami. His strong but gentle hands embraced her. She immediately noticed the flowers because they were her favorite.

"These are for you, beautiful. Hope you like them," he said.

"They are beautiful. How did you know these are my favorite flowers? They smell so good. Thank you."

"You're welcome! But to be honest with you, I didn't know. How was your trip?"

"It was nice."

He reached for her suitcase. "Let me take care of that for you."

"Thanks." She smiled. "The trip was fine, I guess, but I really slept through most of it as soon as the plane took off. But here I am in North Carolina, so I guess you could say okay." She nervously continued to make small talk.

She admired him in silence as he placed her luggage in the car. He was dressed in an all-black tailored suit. Everything about his manner showed power, wisdom, courage, and maturity.

He opened the passenger door then walked behind the car to the driver's side.

"You really look beautiful today. More beautiful than a diamond on a platinum platter," he said.

"You're such a charmer. You're looking very nice yourself. That suit makes you look very distinctive."

"Yeah...you'll tell me anything." He slowed down behind the bright red lights of a police car. "If you don't like it, you can be honest with me."

"Well, at least I know now that you're not stuck up on yourself."

"You ever seen a pretty boy thug?"

"Oh, so you're a thug?"

"Nah, but the government seems to think so," he said as he passed the police car.

"I can't even drive this car most of the time without being pulled over. Those are the real gangsters," he said as he passed the police car. "They are the leading cause of death in the black man's ghetto."

"Oh, and you honestly believe that shit?"

"Yeah, I do!" He suddenly looked her way. She now had his attention with that remark.

"Can you tell me why?" she asked.

"Damn, you sound like you feeling them corrupt gangsters!"

"No, it's not that! It's just that I think we all need law to set the scales of justice. It there's no law, people would be running around like cowboys did back in the day. People would be shooting each other in the back and all."

"Beautiful, they're doing it now," he said as he eased around the curb. "Just think about it with an open mind. Does a piece of paper make it right for one to creep up on a man or woman and kidnap them from their family or home? Because back during slavery, blacks were taken away like that. Now they think it's okay because of a warrant, and most of the time they don't even have evidence to support that shit. They take your house, car, money, computer, and your life. It's nothing but robbery. So, tell me why?"

She sat silent for a moment. "I can't say I totally agree with you. Yes, some cops cross the line, but if they're such gangsters and thugs, why do taxpayers support them?"

"Fear. That's why."

"Fear?" she asked with a hint of strain in her voice. "How did you draw that conclusion?"

"IRS. They extort money to fund the operation. You're a law-abiding citizen, you pay taxes. However, if you don't pay taxes, you're prosecuted. See, people fail to realize that fear is a real scare tactic and strong enough to condition the majority of people to co-operate with the system. Let a black man establish a business and not pay taxes to the government of the United Snakes. He's going directly to prison. But there's a totally different set of laws for the white man."

"So, you researched all this, huh?"

"No! I learned by watching the flow and power of money. It's plain as day."

She really wanted to change the subject. "Can I hear some music, if you don't mind?" She slipped her high heels off and ran her eyes over his muscular body.

"Do you, beautiful. Hope you like Babyface. That's all I have for the moment."

"That's cool." She leaned over to turn on the music.

Damn! he thought to himself as he peeked at her swollen backside. She pretended not to notice him watching.

The scent of her perfume filled his nostrils like a mind-altering aphrodisiac. She adjusted the volume and leaned back in the seat.

"It's so big, Sunami," she said, locking her eyes with his as he raised his head.

"What?" he asked, in shock.

She leaned toward him, stopping her lips only an inch from his ear. "I said, it's so big, Sunami." She paused to allow her words to take effect. "I never touched or handled one as big as the one you're packing."

He was completely caught off guard. She sensed it in his eyes. "How do you know my shit big?" he asked and glanced at her before turning his attention back to the traffic.

"Because I felt it when you hugged me. It was so round and swollen."

He unconsciously looked down to check if there was any truth to her claim.

"Sunami, I'm not talking about your dick!"

"Well, what are you talking about?"

"The gun you have in the holster under your jacket."

He stared at her. She raised her eyebrows, and they both started laughing.

"Aight, you laughing now, but I can't wait to see the look on your face when I go deep in you with it, and check how you come back then. Still got jokes?"

"Oh, I like that one… Let me ask you this, have you ever used your piece to subdue a threat?"

"Damn, you sound like a cop!" he said. "Yeah, all the time."

"Would you take a bullet to protect your friend or someone love?"

"Yeah, if I have to. Honor comes before disloyalty, and honor means you protect your friends and loved ones when you have to."

She never dated a thug and swore years ago, she never would. However, she found herself attracted to him in ways she never felt toward any other man in her life.

His thuggish demeanor was making her wet between her legs. She didn't quite understand why she felt so comfortable around him, but his seductive thuggish power kept her hooked.

"Are you a man strong enough to hold a woman down when she needs to count on you?"

"No question, ma!"

Over the next fifteen minutes, she walked him through the hell of her last two relationships and used the time to help them get better acquainted. He couldn't believe all the emotional suffering she put up with in her past. He couldn't understand why any man would want to hurt, beat, and rape her.

"You don't do that shit to the one you love," he said.

"You're right. Sunami, can you promise me that no matter what happens between us, you will never beat on me or dog me out?"

He turned down the volume on the music. "I'm not gonna sit here and tell you what I think you would like to hear. I wish there was an easy way for me to explain this you, because it's complex. Promises are like spider webs; they trap people into committing themselves for selfish gain. I can promise you a pearl from the well of happiness, but to get there I would probably have to go through a spider web of clustered obstacles. So, I never try to make promises, because they're easy to make and hard to deliver.

"If you have to ask someone for a promise, you have no business trusting that individual. But to answer your question, yes, because I don't believe in beating a woman."

He reminded her of her father in so many ways.

Bright, intelligent, well rounded, and ready to conquer the world. That was good. Now, all she wanted was the man driving her down the highway, leading her to happiness.

Keese

Chapter 10

For more than an hour, Shadow pushed his Humdeville down the streets of Durham. He had made several stops to collect drug money from pushers situated in secluded spots throughout the city that only drug users knew about.

Everlyn moved to the back seat to watch television and to roll a blunt. They were now on their second one since leaving the house.

"Shadow, when are we gonna get something to munch on? I'm hungry as hell!"

"Aight. Let me make this stop over on Rosedale, then we can do that cause I'm hungry as hell, too. You 'bout done with that blunt?"

"Yeah. How much money do y'all make in one day? Y'all niggas getting paid down here." She pushed the button on the remote, sending the TV back into the ceiling of the Hummer, and climbed back into the front seat.

"We make 'bout...half a mill a month," he said while lighting the blunt.

"Right now, me and Sunami are millionaires and thinking about getting out of the game next year. But we don't know just yet."

Her eyes got wide. "Damn, now that's cheddar! Y'all niggas better get out of the game while you can. You know how the streets are. Shit, anything could happen. My father told me years ago the streets are like jackpot slots in a casino... sooner or later, you bound to lose, and usually big time."

"No doubt. Trust, a nigga not gonna be pumping this shit much longer. I'ma gets mine and bounce. Get me a nice house like Sunami and just do it up on some laid-back shit. Na mean?"

"I feel you. So, who you going to see now? Is it our last stop?"

Shadow glanced in the mirror and made a left turn onto Rosedale. "Nah, I got to check this nigga Nickel Bag. That nigga gripped like $125,000 on us last week. Once that's done, we can get something to eat. I got like five spots after we eat, though."

"How y'all niggas let him get $125,000 in the hole like that?"

"We didn't. He claimed he fucked shit up while he was cooking, so we let him ride with that cause he said he could produce our loot back with an extra $125,000. So, we gonna see."

"Okay, what if he doesn't hit you with it? Then what? How do you deal with him?" she asked.

"Shit, I don't know yet. Maybe I let you rock him to sleep. You say we getting it. You can grip money too, if you willing to put work in for it. Be willing to take what you want, causse ain't nobody gonna give it to you," he said while reaching for the blunt. He knew the man had to die if the money wasn't correct.

As far as Shadow's eyes could see were rows of houses on each side of the street. On the far corner was a store with local hustlers standing around, selling drugs to junkies.

"Where are we?" Everlyn asked. She was startled by the sound of a horn blowing.

"This is the hood of the city called The End. I'm gonna be gone for a second. I'll be in that big white house there." He pointed to it and handed her the blunt. She looked down the street at a house about 100 yards away.

"Why you park so far away?"

"Because I don't want police seeing my shit in front of no drug spots. That's how a nigga get hot out here. Just be cool, I'll be right back. Matter of fact, get behind the wheel in case the po-po come through and want you to move or something. They always coming up with some bullshit."

Shadow walked toward the house. He looked around, hyped and alert, checking his surroundings. It was well known by all those undercover cops sat nearby in parked cars watching drug spots before a raid. Once he reached the house, he looked back at Everlyn in the SUV.

Once he reached the top of the stairs, he checked his piece to see if it was positioned to allow him easy draw in case of any threats. He knocked on the door several times.

"What's up, Shadow?" said the tall guy who opened the door. "You kinda early, ain't you?"

Shadow looked Nickel Bag up and down with scrutinizing eyes. He was dressed in black jeans, Tims, and a wife beater. He resembled the singer Keith Sweat.

Nickel Bag was known as a cold-blooded crook throughout Durham. He turned his street corner hustling into a major money-making operation by receiving kilos of cocaine from Shadow and Sunami. He then resold in small quantities and made large profits quickly with a loyal mob of pushers on the streets. Nickel Bag had moved up in the game, earning more money than he could spend.

"What up with you, nigga?" Shadow asked as he entered the house.

"Same shit, different day. I'm just doing it all over again today."

"Who here with you?" Shadow asked as he looked around the empty room.

"Just me now. I'm supposed to have this bitch coming over in a minute, if she shows. But you know how them bitches are."

"I know what you mean. Listen, we need to talk, cousin," said Shadow as they walked down the hall.

"Now you know I'm good. I know I owe Sunami $250,000 already from last week, but y'all gonna have to hold off another week."

Shadow's eyes were expressionless. "What the fuck you mean hold off another week? Nigga, you already two weeks behind. Stop playing! So, now you telling me next week you gonna have $375,000 for us, interest and all?" Shadow started rolling a blunt.

"Nah, I got $80,000 now and I'll hit you with the rest next week. Just tell Sunami let me ride this one last time."

After several moments of silence, Shadow spoke more calmly, "Aight... you got $80,000 now, right?" he said while licking his blunt.

"Yeah, good looking out. I got it in the back."

"No sweat. Don't worry about Sunami. I'll tell him everything's cool. But you gotta come through, my nigga. We done hit you with extra bricks and all we got is $80,000? That's not good." He lit the blunt and stared furiously at Nickel Bag.

"You right! I'ma have it, my nigga!"

"You better, or I'm shutting you down, cause you know the dos and don'ts."

"Man, two of my people got knocked off two weeks ago, and I damn near had to use all my personal money to front a lawyer for them. And you know how legal fees are. So now shit back on track, duke. You feel me?" Nickel Bag took the blunt from Shadow.

"Yeah, you gotta look out for soldiers in this game, cause life is war, love is passion, and anything else fucks up the money," said Shadow.

"Nigga, I like that shit."

"What? The weed?"

"Nah nigga, what you just dropped."

"Oh, you know me. I'm always dropping something."

"Damn, yo! That's some good shit! Where you cop that shit man?"

"This that Yonkers, New York, shit. Me and Sunami went up for the weekend and copped a few pounds to blaze."

"This shit got me fucked up!"

"You gonna be really fucked up in a minute, watch, son."

"Damn!" Nickel Bag looked at Shadow. "It's like that?"

Shadow looked Nickel Bag in the eyes with an intense gaze. "Trust me, you gonna see."

"Man, you a cool ass nigga. You aight by me. That's why I fuck with you the way I do. You keep shit real, and niggas don't even understand that shit."

Shadow was in no mood to hear deceptive words of loyalty. He knew the weed was playing a part of all the bullshit Nickel Bag was kicking. "Real people do real things, and fake ass niggas do fake ass shit in the game."

Shadow pulled hard on the blunt. "I'm saying, niggas think they so slick and don't be knowing most niggas see right through that bullshit they trying to spit. That's why I keep my enemies real close, and friends even closer, because once a friend becomes an enemy, he's even more dangerous."

"You just said some real shit, cousin."

"So, you feel me, right?"

"Hell fucking yeah. A nigga gots to keep it gangster in the streets. That's the only way to keep it, my nigga. Anything else would be fronting."

Shadow suddenly pulled out a large chrome 40 caliber, and his finger was on the trigger. Nickel Bag had a terrified look on his face, and his heart thumped uncontrollably against his rib cage. "Hey, ma...maa...man, what you doing?" he stuttered.

"Nigga, shut the fuck up and get your black ass off that couch before I put a cap in your bitch ass!" Shadow barked.

Nickel Bag sensed his hustling days coming to an end and had no idea how to stop Shadow from killing him.

"Aight, cousin. Don't shoot me. What the fuck is this about?"

"Nigga, I ain't your cousin. Get your ass in the back, bitch. I didn't come to talk." Shadow slapped him across the face with the gun barrel. Nickel Bag screamed loudly and fell backward onto the sofa. Shadow leaned over him and rammed the gun into his mouth so hard that his teeth cracked.

"Aight, now listen to me, motherfucker, and you might live to get revenge. When I tell you to, you gonna get up off your ass, walk that hall to that safe, and empty that stash you got in that closet down there. You hear me, nigga?"

Nickel Bag nodded his head and mumbled.

"Aight, now get the fuck up!" Shadow removed the gun from his mouth, and Nickel Bag struggled to his feet.

"Hurry the fuck up!" said Shadow as he violently pushed him. Nickel Bag stumbled before gaining his balance and pain showed in his face. They both walked toward the bedroom.

When they got into the room, Nickel Bag turned to face Shadow, "Man, why you doing this shit?"

Shadow slapped him before he could finish the last word. "Because you a stupid motherfucker. Never question a man with a gun, fool!" He raised the gun level with his face. "Nigga, don't make me reconstruct your ugly ass face. Get your ass in that closet and open the safe."

Nickel Bag realized that he had a split-second chance. He bent over and slammed his shoulder into Shadow's chest. The force knocked Shadow backward into the television. He grunted loudly as he fought to gain his balance.

Nickel Bag was on him as they both tumbled to the floor. He grabbed Shadow's gun hand by the wrist.

"Yeah, you done fucked up now!" he yelled as he connected a left punch to Shadow's jaw. He drew back in an attempt to land another, as Shadow skillfully stabbed him in the eye with a stiff finger.

"Aaahhh!" Nickel Bag released his grip and covered his eye with both hands. Once his hand was free, Shadow aimed the gun with his finger on the trigger and pulled back.

A flash of fire danced from the cold steel. "Now back the fuck up before the next slug blows your fucking brains out, you stupid ass bitch! You better be heading for that damn closet to open that safe."

Nickel Bag checked his bullet wound and slowly walked to the closet. "Please don't kill me, man." He started crying. "I'm not gonna tell the police, man. Just take it all and let me live. I swear on everything I love. I got a family, man, don't do this."

"Nigga, that nut rag doesn't respect you, but she sure knows how to respect a dick in her mouth. Matter fact, I'ma bang that bitch right after your funeral. Don't fuck with me. Open the damn safe. Now!"

Nickel Bag never imagined he'd actually be robbed and was suddenly disappointed he hadn't concealed some kind of weapon in the closet to protect his worth. Right now, it was some protection he desperately needed.

He slowly dropped to one knee, as if praying. A safe sat on the far-right corner of the back wall. On it was a keypad and small screen. He stared back at Shadow.

"Open that shit, motherfucker!" Shadow yelled and raised his pistol.

The safe could only be opened with a twelve-digit code. Nickel Bag punched in the sequence of numbers. The safe beeped and a green light came on. He slowly opened the heavy steel door.

"Now I've done everything you've asked me to," he said and turned to face Shadow. "Man, please don't kill me. That's all I ask."

Shadow ordered him to back up out of the closet slowly and to sit on the bed. He walked over to the safe and couldn't believe his eyes. He gazed at several kilos of cocaine stacked neatly in a row on the bottom shelf and stacks of money wrapped as if they were done by a bank teller.

"Now what the fuck we got here?" Shadow asked, finding himself confused by the large amounts of cocaine and money. He knew that none of his workers should have this kind of money or coke in their personal possession.

Something wasn't right.

"Nigga, you better explain this shit! You working for someone else?"

Nickel Bag just stared at Shadow.

"Motherfucker, talk. Now!"

Nickel bag spit blood from his busted lip. "Aight, aight. Two weeks ago, a nigga Mellow from the Southside asked me to hold shit for him."

"Mellow? That punk with the twin Denise?" Shadow asked with anger in his voice.

"Yeah...him."

"What the fuck that bitch doing on this side of town asking you to hold him down anyway?"

"I don't know. All he told me was he needed me to hold them bricks for him, and if I didn't, he would have my family killed," Nickel Bag replied.

"You simpleminded motherfucker! You couldn't let me know? You don't let no Southside nigga stash shit in your spot!"

"What the fuck was I supposed to do?"

"Tell that nigga no!"

"When my daughter and girl is under the gun?"

"You should have let us know that nigga was moving in on our turf, that's what! Sunami would've dealt with it," Shadow yelled.

"How the fuck was I supposed to know? The nigga said he had people watching me and my family and if I talked, he would kill them."

"So, where all that money come from? You been pushing weight for that nigga or something?"

"Nah, man. He came over here Saturday night and asked me to hold it. Said some niggas hit his spot, so he needed a new spot to bank his shit."

Shadow was stunned for a second. "Did he say who hit him?"

"No. Man, I'm sorry. I didn't mean it."

"So how come you didn't pump our shit the last two weeks? You holding out on me, motherfucker?" Shadow asked as he raised his gun and searched the scared man's eyes.

Nickel Bag knew there was no correct answer to this question. He looked into the barrel of cold steel with fear. He didn't know what to do.

"Deliver me from my enemies," Nickel Bag mumbled. "O God, defend me from those who rise up against me. Deliver me from the workers of iniquity, and save me from blood-thirsty men, for they lie in wait for my life. They might have now gathered against me," he continued as he thought of his daughter. "Not for all my transgressions nor for my sins, Lord. They run and prepare themselves through no fault of mine. Awake to punish all the nations, don't be merciful to any wicked transgressors."

He cried softly as he whispered Psalm 59.

"Shut the fuck up, nigga! God can't save your black ass. Motherfuckers always crying to God when it's time to die."

Nickel Bag studied Shadow's face in silence and slowly stood to his feet and walked across the room to a dresser.

"Nigga, you ain't crazy! You open that drawer and I'll blast your ass!"

Nickel Bag turned to face him. "You cool…ain't no gun in here. I just want to show you something," he said calmly before carefully pulling the top drawer open. He took out a white envelope and tearfully handed it to Shadow.

Shadow's eyes narrowed as he looked at the small white envelope. "What's in it?"

"Just look, man. Then maybe you'll understand what I'll do for her."

Shadow opened the envelope. Inside were two Polaroids. "Man, what the fuck?!" He found what he was seeing hard to believe.

One photo was of a young girl around five years old with a gun to her head, being forced to perform oral sex on a man. The second photo showed the mother with a gun to her head being forced to watch the gruesome sight.

Nickel Bag noticed that Shadow's facial expression changed to sympathy. "Now do you understand?"

"Man, why the fuck someone doing some shit like this to your daughter?" Shadow asked in disgust. "Yo, that nigga foul. And you a stupid motherfucker for not protecting her! Get your ass up and empty that safe. I hope you didn't think I would feel sorry for your ass."

Shadow spotted two shopping bags and ordered Nickel Bag to fill them with the contents of the safe. Once the bags were filled, he told him to step away from the bags.

"Oh, so now you want to kill me, huh? Rot in hell, motherfucker," Nickel Bag screamed as he rushed Shadow again. Both men struggled for the gun.

Everlyn was growing impatient as she watched *State Property* on the television. Shadow had been gone for more than half an hour. She knew that was more than enough time for him to handle his business and pick up the money. She thought to herself that he was probably in there getting his dick sucked by some nasty ass bitch.

"What's up, cutie?" a young-looking thug asked as he strolled by the Hummer.

"Hey," said Everlyn, simply as a polite response.

He continued walking and got into a yellow mustang and drove off.

A mobster blue Lexus SC 300 on chrome Zenetti rims wrapped in Kumho tires slowly rolled by. Blasting music escaped from the slightly lowered windows, as hidden speakers rattled the trunk.

The car parked directly in front of the house where Shadow was. The driver of the Lexus got out and climbed the stairs to the house. When he reached the top, he pulled a gun from his waist and aimed it forward. His lips were moving rapidly as he spoke to someone Everlyn couldn't see.

She leaned left to right to see who he was holding at gunpoint, but a large tree blocked her view. She couldn't tell what was going on, but she knew she had to find out.

All of a sudden, the thought of Shadow being in danger made her emotional.

She took the keys out of the ignition switch and put them in her pocket. She reached inside her purse and removed the cold steel .380, knowing that there wasn't a moment to waste. She curled her fingers around the trigger, looked at the gun, and a surge of adrenaline shot through her body.

She slowly pulled back the slide. *Wha... chink.* It clicked loudly as it shot forward a center cartridge into the breach. She then got out of the SUV and strutted down the sidewalk toward the house. She put the long strap of the purse over her shoulder. Her hand was inside, snugly wrapped around the gun.

When she reached the stairs, she looked up and saw no one. She climbed the steps, taking them two at a time in her high heels. She quickly scanned the streets below and saw no one, other than a crack head searching the trash cans for something of value. She turned her attention back to the door.

She heard muffled voices on the opposite side of the door. She quickly pulled her ear back, unsure of what to do. She looked around and wondered what Candy would do in this situation.

"Girl, you can't keep no man, cause you like thugs and you can't thug with 'em. If you thug with a nigga, he'll love you for life. A nigga love a down ass bitch." She thought back on the words Candy told her.

Slowly, she turned the doorknob, hoping it would open and praying it wasn't locked. It gave, and the element of surprise was in her favor. She intended to use it to the fullest.

She took a moment to contemplate her own fate, paused, and then said, "Fuck it!" in silence. Her heart thumped erratically in her ear. She swallowed hard as the nervousness caught in her throat.

She was relieved to discover that the muffled voices were coming from the back of the house. She slowly eased the door open and stuck her head through its small crack and looked around.

Her gun was up and close to her cheek. All she saw was an empty hallway. She slipped into the house like a thief and locked the door behind her. She walked nervously down the hall, feeling as if she'd entered a haunted house.

She approached a room and placed her back flush up against the wall and listened to the voices, both of which were now clear to her.

"You crazy motherfucker. You ain't even listening. Half the town is out looking for your black ass. You worth $75,000 right now," said a voice with a deep country accent that Everlyn didn't recognize. "See, like I told you, bro, you ain't took nothing from me. You got the big man, and now he wants you."

"Fuck the big man, the little man, and the damn green giant, cause I ain't take jack from nobody. And I sure as hell don't know what the fuck you talking about!"

Hearing Shadow's voice made Everlyn's heart skip a beat.

She felt like she was no longer in control of her thoughts. She looked around in the room and saw the gunman's back toward her.

Shadow noticed her the moment half her face poked into view. She slipped slowly into the room, carefully pigeon stepping closer to the gunman. Her arms were outstretched and both hands were curled around the .380.

"Say what the fuck you want to say, we'll let the big man decide later."

"Nigga, you 'bout to die," Shadow warned him, "So fuck you, bitch!"

The gunman laughed loudly. "You talk a lot of shit, man. Come, let's go." He waved the gun, motioning Shadow to move.

"Everlyn, smoke this nigga." She quickly pulled her index finger back on the trigger. There was a loud bark, and the .380's slug exploded out the front side of the man's head in a wet pink cloud that splattered Shadow. Before the first shell hit the floor, she let off another round.

The gunman's body collapsed to the floor. Everlyn walked over to the body and looked down. She placed a foot firmly on the back of the man's neck and looked up, locking eyes with Shadow's.

He saw the true dark side of her. She looked demented, cold blooded, and merciless. Is she an evil killer, even more dangerous than Sunami? he asked himself.

Unsure of how to interpret her body language, he willed those thoughts from his mind.

"You alright?" she asked as she walked toward him slowly.

"Thanks to you, I am!" Shadow wiped blood from his face with his shirt tail. She was about to say something when he cut her off. "Damn! Did you have to splatter that nigga all over me?"

"Whatever." She looked around and noticed a second body on the floor. "What the hell happened here?"

"I had a problem and had to handle my business, and then got caught up until you showed up." He pointed to the man she shot. "His name is Mellow. Me and Sunami robbed that fool last week. I'll explain later. Right now, we gots to bounce the hell out of here quick."

They wiped the place clean of all fingerprints, gathered both bags, and exited the house.

"Shadow! We should've picked them shells up!"

He turned to her with a look on his face that said you must think I'm stupid. He looked her in the eyes and said, "I never load a gun without gloves on, so don't even stress that, baby girl."

He smiled and looked at her as if he was reading her thoughts.

Chapter 11

Sunami and Hypnotic drove around Durham sightseeing and getting better acquainted. The exchanged their secrets, past lives, and broken relationships.

There was never an indication of criticism or disapproval, and they felt like they'd known each other all their lives.

Sunami started envisioning what his life would be like with her in it, and that scared him because no woman ever made him feel that way. He wanted her to move in with him, drive his car, and from time to time, even cook his breakfast.

Thoughts of them walking hand in hand through a nice quiet park or along the beach filled his mind. He vowed silently to himself to do just that with her one day.

Hypnotic shared her dream of leaving New York to raise a child or two. She talked about wanting her own home, her own business. The more she spoke, the more she reminded Sunami of the woman he'd always wanted in his life, but never found.

He now felt confident that she was that woman.

During the conversation, Hypnotic was shocked to find out that Sunami had a seven-year-old daughter named Brianna.

Her heart softened more when she found out how devoted he was to his little girl.

He told her about the time he came home from New York and caught Brianna's mother giving head to a guy while the child was asleep, and how he actually forgave her and spent the next two months trying to strengthen their relationship for his daughter's well-being. He tried but fell out of love with her and moved out.

As they rode around the city, Hypnotic took in its beauty. They passed huge homes with well-manicured lawns. She ooowed and ahhhed along the way, praying one day have her own.

She noticed how women gazed at her, Sunami, and the Ferrari. Their eyes showed respect and a hint of envy. Suddenly, hunger took control of Sunami's stomach.

He searched for a place to wine and dine.

"Hypnotic," he whispered under soft music.

"Huh?" she said, snapping out of her daydream.

"What's up?"

"Are you hungry? I know a nice Cuban spot, not far from here."

"Will this be like a date, or is it a friendly thing?" he asked, as she gazed at him with a charming smile.

He evaluated the look on her face, trying to read her intentions. Keith Sweat sang, *you may be young, but you're ready... ready to learn*, as if coaching him on.

"Friends don't date," he replied. "So, let's make it a date that's in search of friendship."

"You know what that means, right?"

"What?"

"It means that if this date for any given reason don't go right, you don't get a kiss, boner, extra point, or whatever you men always seem to think you should get after a date."

"Oh, you got jokes, huh?" They both laughed.

"We'll see about that...with your fine ass. Seeing how you wanna drop all these stipulations on a brother, can I drop one on you just to make things more interplayable?"

"Oooo...interplayable...big word! Do you always go big?"

"You think you slick?"

"What?" she said with an innocent voice, knowing he read her.

"You're avoiding the question."

"What is it?"

"Like you said, if the date doesn't go right, I get no kiss or the man in the boat. I can handle that...no sweat. But for you, you'll have to sleep in bed with me butt ass naked!"

"Now that's dirty, and you know you ain't right."

"I'm saying, if I must suffer so should you."

"Okay, deal. How's the food at this restaurant? Good?"

"Yeah! It's a Cuban joint on the south side, candlelit tables and French windows... the whole nine yards. The food is excellent."

"Seems romantic. Will I be the first lady you've taken to this place?"

"No."

She sat upright in her seat, not liking how he said that. She didn't want to be taken to some place he'd taken all his other dates.

"Relax. The only other woman I've taken to this place is my daughter. We go there for a bite to eat cause she can't stand McDonald's."

"Who's that? I never met a kid that didn't like their food."

"Well, my baby doesn't. She says it don't taste right."

"Okay, she's got good taste."

"Just like her daddy, I guess," he teased.

He pulled into the parking lot and cautiously backed between two cars.

He got out of the car and walked over to the passenger side to open the door for her. As she stood up, he noticed how her skirt clung to her thick thighs and ass.

He wrapped his arm around her waist and led her toward the entrance of the restaurant. When they reached the door, they had to jump back to avoid being knocked over by four men walking out like a gust of wind.

"Mario, we're still in the blind concerning this whole mess," said one of the men in a Cuban accent.

"Nobody knows nothing and claims to have seen nothing."

Mario responded, "Then do what needs to be done. Find his family."

The men were so wrapped up in their conversation that they didn't even see Sunami and Hypnotic. Hypnotic was appalled by their rudeness and couldn't help but study each man's face and words for the brief moment of this encounter.

Once inside, she looked around and noticed that the place was packed with couples enjoying their evening.

The sound of clinking glasses filled the air, and the soft lighting set the place with a romantic mood.

A hostess approached them. "Just two?" the hostess asked.

"Yes," said Sunami.

"Okay, this way please." As the hostess led them toward a table, Sunami watched Hypnotic's ass as it bounced up and down under her tight skirt. He also noticed other men staring too.

"Were you watching my ass again?"

"Of course! Me and every man in here, not to mention some of the ladies too!"

She shook her head. "You something else, with your young ass."

"Is that a complaint? Cause you ain't seen nothing yet, baby."

"Nah, I'm just amazed at how attractive you find me. I mean, I am nine years older than you," she said.

"That shouldn't amaze you! You are very beautiful."

"I don't know, sometimes I find myself struggling with my age, and lately I've gained a few pounds and—"

He cut her off, "who told you that? I really like it, so it had to be some evil ass woman hating on you, because you are all that! Ain't no nigga in his right mind told you no crazy shit like that there!"

"Tell me anything, you just trying to win the bet."

"On the real, shorty, I'm feeling you, so don't get me twisted with them other niggas. If I wasn't feeling you, then you wouldn't have gotten my credit card number or my undivided attention. My baby mama didn't even get those numbers…and I'm gonna win the bet."

"She has your child, why not?"

"Because I don't trust her scandalous ass. Once someone betrays me, there's nothing left to be desired and all trust ceases. Especially her, because she'll sell her own mama for a silk stocking." They both burst out in laughter.

"So, how does she feel about you?"

He was silent for a moment. His daughter's mother almost ruined his life. She threatened to turn him in to the police for a murder. Instead, she blackmailed him for ten grand a month in exchange for her silence. "She doesn't love me; she loves my money! Real love is sacrifice sometimes, and she's never been willing to make a sacrifice for me."

"That can't be true. She had your daughter. You must have some feelings for her, right?"

"Having a child don't make you a woman or a man, only a mother or father. Shit, she can't even get that correct. All she cares about is getting high right now. You think the courts care? They don't give a fuck. I must go through all the proper steps to prove that she's an unfit mother. So, for two years, I've been dealing with them social service bastards and courtroom imperialists."

She looked into his eyes, now knowing how hurt he really was. "I know dealing with social services can be stressful, so if what you say about your daughter's mother is true, I don't see why they won't let you get full custody."

"Sunami, if there's anything I can do to help, let me know."

"Thanks, I appreciate your concern. I'm just tired of all the courtroom bullshit and will be so glad when it's all over."

"Excuse me, are you two ready to order?" asked a waitress approaching their table.

"Yes, we are. How are you doing?" Sunami asked the long-haired, thick-hipped waitress.

"Working hard, as always. You know how it is when you got bills and a little one to feed."

"I know that's right."

The waitress gazed at Hypnotic and then looked off.

"So, you finally decided to give dating a try, huh?" the waitress stated more than asked.

"Excuse me. Hypnotic, this is Sandria. Sandria, this is Hypnotic."

"Nice to meet you," Hypnotic said in a soft voice as she shook the woman's hand.

"You too. She's beautiful, Sunami. You're a lucky man."

"Thanks, Sandria. You ain't never lied!"

"How is your daughter?"

"She's fine."

"Have you met his daughter yet?" Hypnotic shook her head. "She is the most adorable little girl, especially when she's mad."

Hypnotic chuckled as the waitress gave details about how Sunami interacts with his daughter. She was finding out that he was a devoted father and was telling the truth about not bringing other women to the restaurant.

Since he was so used to being single, Hypnotic figured he was in search of love and affection in his life.

Their casual conversation continued during the meal. They both ate very quickly, which could have been taken as a clue to how hungry they were for one another.

"Now that was a meal. I haven't had a pie that thick ever in my life," she said as she licked her lips.

"I'm glad you enjoyed it, beautiful. Hope you're not too full, because you might want to get stuffed later on tonight," he said as he looked into her eyes

"What makes you so sure of that?"

So, you think you can read me that well?"

"Nah, but you can't front on me. I've known you wanted me ever since I heard—"

"Here's your drinks." The waitress interrupted before Sunami could finish his sentence. The waitress placed a bottle of champagne and glasses on the table and walked off.

"Now, as you were saying before we were interrupted?" Hypnotic said as she stared at him with an inquisitive grin.

"Never mind."

"No, tell me. I want to hear what you have to say."

"I forgot."

"Yeah, I bet you did."

After a few glasses of champagne, they were both tipsy and turned on.

"Will you drive for me?" he asked. "I'll guide you to my house."

"Say no more. I need to go to the ladies' room first."

She stood up and walked toward the bathroom. She could feel his gaze upon her ass. She glanced back at him, and from the look on her face, she felt entirely naked.

When she got to the ladies' room and into a stall, she put her hand between her thighs and was surprised how soaked her panties were. She took them off, put them in her purse, and returned to the table.

"You ready? Let's get out of here, baby."

"What took you so long?" he asked.

"I'm a woman... patience is a virtue."

Sunami paid the bill and they exited the restaurant.

Hypnotic looked across the hood at Sunami as she opened the driver's side door. "Why you tip her so much?"

"I always tip her big. I owe her for looking out for me once." He smiled. Hypnotic had no idea that her drink had been spiked with Red Cell, a substance ten times stronger than Spanish Fly.

"I don't know what it is about you, Sunami, but I'm fucking your ass tonight, and I don't ever give up any pussy on the first date."

Keese

Chapter 12

Hypnotic raced the black Ferreri in and out of traffic like a stealth racing to war. She ignored some traffic lights and signs.

"Damn! Slow this bitch down before po-po gets behind your ass. You ain't in the Bronx!"

"Relax, you'll be okay," she responded. "You're not afraid of my driving, are you?"

"Nah!"

"Good, Cuz you ain't seen nothing yet."

"See those light right there, that's my house. Pull in."

Hypnotic saw the house and screamed. "Oh my god! Sunami, your house is beautiful!"

She drove up the long winding driveway and then pulled into the garage. "Quite an impressive collection of automobiles you got here."

Sunami thanked her, gathered her bags, and disarmed the alarm system.

When they entered the house, she looked around and was even more astonished by the luxurious kitchen with stainless steel appliances, black sinks, black marble countertops, and cherry wood cabinets.

"So, you feeling my shit, huh?"

"It's a beautiful kitchen," she said while eyeing the ceiling fans. "Everything smells so new in here. You just remodeled or something?"

"No! Been like that for the past three years. Come on, I'll show you the rest of the house, and then I'll show you, my bedroom." Hand in hand, they both entered the large living room.

"You don't watch TV in here?" she asked.

He strolled over to the sofa, lifted a remote, and pressed a button, and the television lowered from its hiding place in the ceiling. "How's that?" he said.

She had never seen a home this beautiful and wondered why his child's mother would toss the chance to live in such luxury. She pictured herself awakening every morning in this home. Sunami continued their tour of the house, taking her from room to room.

"Now let me show you where you'll be sleeping tonight," he said.

As they walked into the bedroom, she saw a bed that looked big enough to sleep four giants.

His nostrils filled with her fragrance as their eyes met. She stared at him in silence.

"I'm going downstairs to bring your things up. You want something to drink?"

"All I want to drink is you," she responded as she stepped closer to him. She leaned in to kiss him.

His hands slid down her back and cupped her big, round ass.

She moaned and worked on loosening his belt buckle. She kissed and undressed him simultaneously. She kissed him on his neck, behind his ears, and up and down his chest as she removed his jacket, gun, and shirt.

Together, they undressed each other. She led him to the bed and suddenly pushed him backward on it. She stepped forward and leaned in between his legs.

"Damn," she said. She was frightened by the length of his dick. There was no way in hell he could put all that up in her. She would have to do the driving.

Sunami moaned as she wrapped her hands around the base and licked the head and length with the tip of her tongue. He closed his eyes as the look of surrender masked his face. *I'm gonna turn this young motherfucker out*, she thought to herself.

She wrapped her warm, full lips around the head and took him in inch by inch. She almost choked as she felt him in the hollow of her throat. She removed his manhood from her mouth and looked into his eyes.

Thinking she was uncomfortable or something was wrong, he expressed sincerely, "You don't have to if you don't want to."

She placed a finger to her lips. "Shhh." She licked her lips and blew her warm breath on the head of his dick.

She licked it until it was completely wet and brick hard.

She teased his testicles with the tip of her tongue and sucked them into her mouth. She gradually worked her way back to the shaft. She stroked and sucked him into a frenzy.

Suddenly, loud footsteps could be heard racing up the stairs. "Brittany and Brianna been kidnapped, cousin!"

Shadow yelled loudly.

Sunami jumped out of the bed when Shadow and Everlyn burst into the room. He was stark naked and couldn't believe what he was hearing.

"Nigga, you better stop playing with me! You know I don't play no games when it comes to my daughter," he screamed, as Hypnotic ran into the bathroom.

"He's for real, Sunami," Everlyn said with seriousness in her voice.

The life quickly drained from Sunami's face. His legs weakened, and he dropped down on the bed. "How did you find out, and how do you know Brittany ain't playing games?"

"Because whoever got them called me on my cell phone. I went out to Brittany's house and her car was there, but they were nowhere to be found."

"What did the caller say?" Sunami wanted to know word by word. He got dressed quickly. "Did he say what time he would call back or what he wanted?"

"Nah." There was silence for a second. "The nigga sounded Spanish."

"Spanish! You ever given your number to a Spanish guy?"

"Not this number."

"What the fuck! It's gotta be someone who knows us. Got to be."

"I doubt that," Shadow said bluntly.

"Why you say that?"

"Because a nigga that know you would've never done no crazy shit like that, knowing you would kill them. Niggas know how we do."

Keese

Chapter 13

An hour and half later, Sunami and Shadow sat on the step at Brittany's house. They had frantically searched the house thoroughly for any indication of who may have kidnapped them.

The house was ransacked, furniture destroyed, and his daughter's dog decapitated. Its head sat at the bottom of the aquarium he bought for her last birthday.

An older, slender lady across the street noticed both men on the step. She strolled over toward them. "You two out mighty late tonight."

Sunami raised his head and recognized the woman.

He had slept with her a few times in the past and helped her with her rent.

"What's up, Ms. Story? You alright tonight?"

"That's what I came to ask you."

After a moment of silence, Sunami asked, "What would make you think something's wrong?"

"Because I find it odd y'all sitting out here like this."

Sunami could no longer hold back his emotions and broke down in a storm of tears. Ms. Story sat down and wrapped her arms around him to help him calm down. Once he calmed down, he nervously explained everything to her.

She wanted to tell Sunami and Shadow what she saw, but was afraid that the men who kidnapped Brittany and Brianna would come back for her if she said anything. Ms. Story loved little children, and knew deep down in her heart she wouldn't be able to live with herself if she remained silent.

"Sunami, when I came outside to water the plants today, I saw a white Lexus and a black Range Rover parked in front of this house. Two men got out and knocked on the door. I saw Brittany at the door talking to them for a few minutes. Then both men bust up into the house like two angry devils."

She paused and took a deep breath. "Then they came out. Brittany looked really mad, and that little angel of yours was yelling at both of them devils like she was god. Both men pushed them into the Range Rover and they raced outta here like they were the A-Team."

"Have you ever seen those guy's cars over here before?" Sunami asked.

"Nope."

"Did they see you, Ms. Story?" Sunami asked with concern.

"I reckon, but I can't say for sure though."

After a moment's pause, Sunami glanced over at Shadow and then looked her in the face. "Ms. Story, I don't know these guys and they might try coming back to see you later. I think you should come stay with me for a while to be safe."

Worry quickly masked the woman's face. She hadn't been feeling right since she witnessed it anyway.

"Just until things get cleared up. You don't have to worry about food, about anything. I'll take care of you."

"Can I bring Fuzz?" she asked.

"Sure, your cat can come."

Ms. Story packed a few things, put her cat in a carrier, and got into Shadow's Hummer. She tried her best to describe the men. Sunami and Shadow figured these dudes were from the Southside.

When they arrived at Sunami's house, he took Ms. Story to his guest bedroom. Shadow, Hypnotic, and Everlyn gathered around the sofa.

"You okay, baby, anything I can do for you?" Hypnotic asked Sunami as he entered the living room.

"Don't worry about me. Somebody better worry about those bitches who took Brianna and her mother."

"Sunami, you gotta calm down. I know your mad right now, but yelling is not the answer. We'll find your daughter."

Shadow's cell phone rang. "Might be them!"

Shadow answered the phone.

Mario paced back and forth across the floor. He turned to face a blind-folded woman. Her hands were handcuffed.

"Bitch, I'm gonna ask your filthy ass one more time, where does your boyfriend live?"

The woman squirmed in the cuffs. "Please, I told you I don't know what you're talking about."

He violently slapped her across the face. She spit blood from freshly torn wounds to her mouth and lip.

"When Sunami finds you, he's going to kill you!" Two men had already raped and tortured her.

"Bitch, where's the bastard and my money?" He slapped her again.

"Fuck you!" She started crying and laughing at the same time. "You don't scare me, fuck you!"

He stared at her in frustration. She wasn't going to talk and he knew that. He walked toward the door, reached for the knob, and snatched it open. "Bring me the little bitch!"

A large man entered the room and led the little girl in.

"Hey there. What's your name, little one?"

"Brianna," she responded.

"Baby, don't say nothing to him," yelled Brittany.

"Why you do that to my mommy?"

"She'll be okay. I'm trying to help. Listen, Brianna, your mother is hurt really bad and we need to find your daddy. Do you know his phone number?"

"It's 544-4326. Are you gonna call him?" She had given the man Shadow's number.

"Yes, I am, sweetheart. Would you like to talk to him?"

She nodded her head.

Mario pulled out his cell phone and dialed the number.

"Yeah," the voice on the receiving end said flatly.

"Is Sunami tied up at the moment?"

"Who's calling?" Shadow asked.

"This is Mario with a very urgent call. It's concerning life and death. Whose life depends on him and how well he listens."

"He's not in right now. He's out searching for your dead ass!"

"You listen to me! If he wants to see Brianna again, you need to listen to what the fuck I tell you! Just tell Sunami and Shadow to meet me on Lakewood Avenue by Roseview School tomorrow at 9 a.m. Tell him I want the four million dollars they stole from by brother by Sunday morning. Make sure they show tomorrow morning. I'll have a little something for them."

He handed the phone to Brianna. "Daddy!"

"Hey, baby, this is your uncle Dwight. Are you okay?"

"I wanna go home!"

"I'ma come get you. Me and your daddy. Is your mommy, okay?"

"She bleeding and crying. Tell my daddy that!"

Mario snatched the phone from her and disconnected the call.

Sunami, Hypnotic, and Everlyn stood around in silence as Shadow spoke on the phone.

"That was the Spanish dude you told me about, wasn't it?" Sunami asked.

"Yeah, that was that motherfucker."

"What he say?"

"He said he wanted the four million dollars we stole from him."

Hypnotic studied the men's faces and knew her back was against the wall. She had to tell them about her past life. "Sunami, may I speak with you in private, please?"

He studied her face for a moment. "Aight." He then turned to Shadow. "Call Scar, Bullet, and Passion. Tell them what's going down and to meet me in the conference room, ASAP."

"Say no more. Done deal, cousin."

"And call Outlaw. I need him here by morning."

He turned and walked toward Hypnotic and motioned for her to step outside by the pool. He opened the glass door, and they stepped out into the cool air of the night. "What's up, beautiful?"

She didn't want to bring any more difficulty to his life, and she had no idea how he would react to her secret.

"Sunami, there's something I've been wanting to tell you." Her eyelids fluttered involuntarily as if she was about to cry.

"I hope like hell you not about to tell me you used to be a man or something."

"Hell no!" she yelled in a thick New York accent.

"What then? Just say it, baby. Ain't nothing can be worse than my daughter and her mother missing, so spit it out."

She took a deep breath. "A year ago, me and my ex-boyfriend was fooling around with his new digital camera. One thing led to another and we ended up taking pictures of each other. Six months later we had a nasty fight, and I told him that I no longer wanted to deal with him. Well, he was a sore loser and decided to get even by putting those nude pictures of me on the internet. Because of that, I was fired from my job."

"That's fucked up, but that's cool with me."

"Sunami...I used to be a cop. A detective for the department..."

"A fucking cop? Bitch, you got five seconds to tell me why I shouldn't kill your ass right now!" his voice thundered and startled everyone in the house.

"Sunami, what the hell are you doing?"

Sunami was aiming his monstrous .44 caliber between Hypnotic's eyes. "Sunami, take a deep breath. You don't have to do this. We can talk." She raised her hand and slowly showed her palms. "I think I know who Mario is. Let me help you!"

Sunami just looked at her with a confused, angry, and puzzled expression. As Shadow and Everlyn walked outside, Sunami briefly looked away at them. When he did, Hypnotic spun around, raised Sunami's arm over her shoulders and flipped him over into the pool.

"Bitch, are you crazy!" Sunami shouted.

"You were the one with the gun. I had to do something."

Everyone looked at Hypnotic with their mouths hung wide open.

"How do you know who he is?" he asked as he climbed out of the pool.

"Do you remember those guys that almost knocked us down at the restaurant?"

"Yeah, I remember those assholes. We ain't never stole no money from that nigga!"

"What the hell y'all talking about?" Shadow asked.

Hypnotic turned to face him. "Sunami and I ran into him at that Cuban joint. Him and some other guys almost knocked us down coming out the door. I remember one of the guys addressing another one as Mario."

"We ain't never robbed no Cuban motherfuckers for four million dollars!" said Shadow.

"Maybe not, cousin, but that faggot thinks we did," said Sunami.

"Which gives us leverage to get your daughter and her mother back. If he's under the impression you took his money, we can use that to your advantage," said Hypnotic.

Everlyn looked puzzled. "How they gonna do that?"

Hypnotic thought about her question for a second and suddenly came up with an idea. "Tell me exactly what Mario said to you, Shadow."

"The same thing I told Sunami already."

"Did he say when he wanted the money?"

"By Sunday morning, and to meet him tomorrow morning at 9 a.m. on Lakewood Avenue by Roseview School. Said he had a little something for us, and if we didn't show, he'd kill Brianna the way he killed her dog."

"He didn't say anything about how you should drop the money off?"

"Nah, he didn't even know who I was and said to tell Sunami that."

"Good. That should give us a chance to even the odds a little here," Hypnotic said with a slight smile. "Let's go inside and talk some more. I'm sure you all will agree once I tell you what's on my mind."

They went inside and waited in the living room while Sunami changed into dry clothes.

Ms. Story was cleaning and dusting. "Can I get y'all anything? Like a snack or a drink?" she asked.

"You know how to mix drinks?" Shadow asked.

"Youngin', Redd Foxx ain't got nothing on old Ms. Story. Is there a special kind of drink you want, son?"

"Yeah, can you make a Green Hornet?"

"Sure can." She looked up toward the ceiling.

Everyone studied this attractive, slender, older woman. She was 5'9" with large breasts and a flat stomach. Her hair was cut neat and short.

"Now I remember. Been a while since I bartended. That would be two ounces of Intrigue, one ounce of premium tequila, with a splash of pineapple juice to give it a nice mellow taste. One Green Hornet coming up. You two want something?"

Everlyn asked for a Purple Passion and Hypnotic asked for a Santa Sandria.

Ms. Story served them the drinks and took a seat beside Hypnotic.

"Thank you, Ms. Story, you're a very nice person," said Hypnotic.

"You are too, even though you took my man," she said jokingly. "You really like him, don't you?"

Hypnotic nodded a yes, while sipping her drink.

Sunami came into the living room, wearing a wife beater and shorts. He went over to the bar and made a drink.

"Now what's the plan you came up with, Hypnotic?"

She carefully advised them on the best course of action and left out none of the details. She let them know that she'd used this plan before on a kidnapping case in New York.

"Are you sure this will work, Hypnotic?" Shadow asked.

"Man, that motherfucker might shoot us the minute he sees us."

"Stop thinking like that!" said Everlyn.

"It'll all work. All we got to do is play our parts right."

Spending a moment to play all that Hypnotic had placed in his mind, Sunami turned to Shadow. "Okay, did you make the call like I asked you to?"

"Yeah. Outlaw is on his way now. And I called the others. They should be here real soon."

"Aight, cool. Take Everlyn with you and get everything we need. Don't half step. Radios, bulletproof vests, guns, silencers, the whole works. We ain't playing with these bastards."

Hypnotic was stunned. "You have hardware like that on hand?"

"Yeah... why?"

"Can I have a look?"

"You're not gonna arrest me later, are you, Ms. Detective?"

"Not a chance. I'ma need to check your rifles when we get back."

"Back from where?" he asked with a raised brow.

"We need to go check out this Lakewood Avenue in advance to see the layout, then I can tell you even more and get my brother to bring everything else we need."

"What the hell you up to, shorty?"

"Nothing. I just want to make sure we get your daughter back with her mother in one piece."

Chapter 14

Outlaw arrived first, followed by Scar, Bullet, and Passion. They were all briefed about the kidnapping.

Hypnotic advised every one of her plans and wanted to make sure that everyone knew and followed their role precisely.

Each person wore lightweight Kevlar vests under their clothing. Each member also had a 5.6 Bores, which were slightly larger than an M-16. They each also had hideaway holsters at their hips with Glock 19s equipped with power sights, slide-lock back button clip ejection, and MX502 silencers.

For additional protection, each one had a palm-sized, 45-caliber combat Mark Master 1 automatic strapped to their ankles.

"Aight, is everybody ready to do this?" Sunami asked.

"I want everybody to remember their roles and be precise with it," said Hypnotic. "If there's anyone who don't know their role, please speak up now so we can correct any mistakes before they're made."

They were now ready to roll out. Hypnotic was disappointed because her brother hadn't arrived yet.

Everlyn tried to comfort her. "You'll be okay, girlfriend. We got your back on this."

"I know, but I don't understand why he didn't make it. It's not like him. He's always here for his big sis."

"You alright, beautiful?" Sunami said to her more than asking. He watched as she sat on the sofa checking her gun.

She held an Armelo BGR 300 Winchester magnum sniper's rifle, equipped with a powerful 10x42 scope.

"Are you sure you can handle that?" he asked.

"That bitch got crazy kick to it."

"I turn you on, don't I?"

"Here we are 'bout to set it off like the Fourth of July and you two on some J. Lo and Wesly Snipes shit," said Outlaw as he loaded his dump pouches with extra clips.

There was a brief conversion between them all.

They discussed the plan to make sure everyone was on point and ready to handle business.

No one knew what to expect or how the kidnappers would react. They all took separate cars and agreed to allow nothing or no one to derail their plans. Including the police.

Sunami dressed down in death black swat fatigues with cargo pants. He stood in front of his gun smoke-gray Hummer and looked around while he pulled on a blunt. Morning traffic moved up and down the street. He glanced at his watch and wondered when the kidnappers would show.

"Watch where you're going, you big jerk!" a lady with a shopping cart overloaded with trash yelled to a woman in her car as she shuffled through busy traffic and crossed the street.

Sunami placed his finger to his ear against the flesh-colored device snuggled inside and spoke into his watch, asking if anyone had seen anything. They all wore wireless communication devices similar to those used by the FBI.

Hypnotic was 500 yards away, hidden well out of view on top of a building. She looked through her scope and searched the traffic.

"This is H-3. Nothing!" she whispered. When Sunami heard her voice, he smiled as he thought of how he had actually found a real trooper in her.

"P-7, how you looking?" he asked Passion.

"P-7 in position." Passion was parked in a white Mercedes two blocks away.

"O-5, you good, cousin?"

"Locked and loaded," Outlaw assured everyone. He was sitting four blocks away on his red CBR.

"That's my nigga. E-4, you ready?"

Everlyn responded as she sat in Shadow's Humdeville a block away.

"Ms. 9, I see you...looking good."

"This shit smells, boy. I'm doing this for Brianna now, not you!" said Ms. Story.

"S-6, what's poppin'?"

112

"Nothing yet, but my gun will soon," said Scar, who was hidden nearby behind a car.

"Man, you ain't never lied. B, what's going on?"

"Little nervous, but it's all good," Bullet responded.

"S-2, it's now me and you."

"I'm ready," Shadow said from the passenger side of his Humdeville.

"A white stretch limo and blue Lincoln just passed me," said Outlaw.

"Copy, O-5. Stand by, everyone, this could be them," said Hypnotic.

The clean stretch limo with dark tinted windows rounded the corner and entered the parking lot, stopping a few feet away from Sunami's Hummer.

A tall, thin, bald white man wearing a large diamond hoop earring and a patch over his eye got out from the driver's side. He walked to the back of the limo and stood there.

Suddenly, the back doors flung open and two henchmen popped out, followed by a Cuban man in a pair of snakeskin boots.

"Daddy!" Brianna yelled but was cut off by the closing of the door.

Sunami's heart raced with fear that his daughter would be harmed. However, he remained calm and acknowledged his gangster ability and heart as the Cuban guy approached.

"You Sunami?"

Sunami stared deeply into the man's eyes. "And you are?"

"My name is Mario. Are you Sunami?"

"Yes, I am. What do my daughter and her mother have to do with you?"

The man studied Sunami's facial expression and spoke slowly. "I can see that you're a man who likes to get directly to the point. So let me be as direct as possible so there's no misunderstanding."

"Like what?"

"You see, for the past two years, you've managed to accumulate a great deal of money at the expense of my brother and me by killing and robbing my people. If the money isn't returned in full, I assure

113

you, I will break and enter your daughter's vagina. Then I'm gonna personally kill the little bitch. You do see how easy it is to locate your family?"

Shadow was infuriated by the man's threats against Brianna. He jumped out of his Hummer and stepped toward the man, "Mother-fucker, you touch one hair on my niece's head and I'll personally slaughter your whole family and everything you love! Me and my nigga ain't never took jack from you or your punk ass brother. You got shit twisted."

Hypnotic heard the conversation. She looked through her scope and zeroed in on Mario's forehead. She weaved the rifle around, bringing everyone into view while conducting a dry run, then returned to Mario. His head was directly between her crosshairs.

"H-3 clear with two shots," she said with small beads of sweat on her forehead. "You confirm and I'll drop this bastard right now."

"Stand down," Sunami said as he seized Shadow by the arm and spoke indirectly to Hypnotic.

"Standing down," she responded.

Sunami inhaled deeply. "Shadow, get back inside and maintain."

He turned to Mario. "What makes you so sure we're the ones who robbed you?"

"We've known about you for some time now, but you see, we had no way of proving it until recently. We both know you're the men who took our money. Best you return it for the safety of your daughter. Do we have an understanding?"

Sunami looked to the sky as if praying for Brianna and Brittany's safety. This was his hint to Shadow for their next move.

Shadow knew that they only had seconds until the next plan. They had to move quick, fast, and silently. "Ms. 9," he began with orders, "B-8 and S-6, Brianna is in the back of the limo. Let's get to rocking y'all!"

Scar crouched down low and dashed through parked cars, silently threading his way toward the blue Lincoln as Bullet did the same. Both men held guns ready, looking forward to the gun fight that was about to erupt.

"B-8 in position," Bullet whispered only inches away from the back door of the Lincoln.

"S-8 in position, at the trunk of the Lincoln," Scar said.

"Ms. 9, you ready?" Shadow asked.

"Sure am," Ms. Story responded back.

"Do what you do best then."

Ms. Story made way across the parking lot, pushing the shopping cart out of control as Sunami spoke with Mario. She was feeling nervous and fearful, which played a part in her enacting what she was about to pull off. She knew that what she was about to do was dangerous, but was, in fact, the right thing to do, and she couldn't fail.

"Ask to see Brianna," Hypnotic stated as she zeroed in on the limo's rear window. "I can take out those in back, if need be, but I need that window down."

Anger curled the corner of Sunami's mouth and all about his face. "May I see my little girl? How do I know you haven't killed her already?"

Mario turned slightly and looked over his shoulder.

"Lower the window and allow the girl to speak to her daddy."

The window lowered halfway down. "Daddy! Daddy!" Brianna yelled.

"I want to go home, Daddy!"

The sound of her voice brought on feelings in Sunami that only a father could feel as he looked through the window and saw her sitting between two men with weapons. His heart thumped as he realized he couldn't possibly let Hypnotic take a shot.

"I have both men in view," she said calmly, as she curled her finger on the trigger.

Sunami stepped directly into the line of fire.

"What are you doing?" she asked angrily.

"Can't let you," he responded. He was afraid she would miss and endanger his daughter.

A loud boom suddenly thundered through the air. Mario's henchmen were disoriented and jumped nervously.

Two of the men jumped from the car and reached for the weapons. Ms. Story had slammed the shopping cart into the limo's side. She mumbled loudly at the cart, as if she was speaking to a cat.

"Jesus, lady, for Christ's sake, why don't you watch where you're pushing that thing?" one of the men blasted. "You dented my car, you crazy ass bitch!"

"You should have listened to me," she said, pointing her finger at the cart. "You always running off every time I feed you. That's why you can't go everywhere I go. Shoulda never let my husband conduct that stupid brain surgery on you."

"You're a nut, lady," the Cuban said. "Go on, get out of here!"

Bullet and Scar quickly sprung into action as the second man stood by laughing at Ms. Story. Bullet rolled under the car and attached a little black box to its gas tank.

He pressed a button, activating the red light on the device.

"B-8 completed," he whispered.

Shadow hadn't heard from Scar. "S-6, you in position, you copy?" Scar had just reached his position and opened the back door of the car and placed a black box under the seat.

He switched it on and quietly closed the door. "S-6 in position, you copy?"

"Copy that. Now both of you hurry up and bounce," Shadow ordered.

Sunami smiled to himself because Hypnotic's plan was working well so far. He listened well while he spoke with Mario.

"I noticed something very peculiar about you that I don't quite understand. Why you always smiling, young man?" Mario asked him.

"Motherfucker, I was growling, not laughing. When this is all over with, you and your brother will realize heaven was never hard to find."

"If I had a nickel for every threat promised me, I would have retired ten years ago. My advice to you, young man, is that you gather my brother's money up so I can collect, or I'll ship your daughter to you piece by fucking piece. That's no threat, that's a damn fact." Mario reached into his coat, pulled out a CD, and handed it to Sunami.

"What the fuck is this? Does it tell me how to drop the money off?"

"No! We'll contact you with that information. That there is a... how do you say it? A little something, something for you, man." Mario laughed and motioned to the man with the patch over his eye, who then walked to the rear of the Lincoln with two other men and opened the trunk.

They struggled with something. Seconds later, they tossed Brittany's lifeless body on the ground.

Sunami's heart stopped. He had to fight the urge to scream. Tears rolled down his cheek and his lips twitched uncontrollably.

He slowly turned around and looked into the early morning sky. He widened his eyes and spoke as if he was speaking to God. "If anything happens to me, please take care of my daughter."

Hypnotic curled her finger around the trigger.

"Please be careful," she whispered, as she zeroed the crosshairs in on Mr. One Eye. "S-6 and B-8, get in that limo as fast as you can. I'ma down both men behind Mario. Shadow, be ready to move."

"S-6 in position, locked and loaded," said Scar.

"B-8 in position, locked and loaded," said Bullet.

"On my one, everybody," Hypnotic whispered.

"Three, two..." She was lying on her stomach as she inhaled slowly applied pressure to the trigger. "One." She pulled the trigger back twice. The powerful gun kicked back against her shoulder.

The first slug smashed into the man's eye and exploded internally. As the force lifted him and slammed him against the side of the car, his face exploded into a gray, purple, and red misty cloud.

The second man took a bullet to the shoulder that spun him around wildly. Dark blood spouted from his large wound.

The back door of the limo opened, and the most attractive woman dove out and rolled to her feet. She crouched low on one knee and held her weapon before aiming.

Sunami sprung into action by pulling his gun from its holster as Mario kicked him behind the knee, causing him to stumble and fall.

Mario quickly sprinted toward the limo. Bullet and Scar sprinted into action as the two Cubans fell. Both men aimed at the remaining Cubans and held their triggers down as the truncated cylinder attached to their barrels spit into action.

The 5.66 mm assault rifles jerked in their hands, slamming the stocks back and forth in their stomachs like jackhammers out of control.

"Lord, have mercy!" screamed Ms. Story. She left the cart behind and raced toward the two parked cars and ducked for cover.

Movement down below caused Hypnotic to weave her gun back and forth. She nervously tried to zero in on the target. But there was so much movement and she couldn't risk hitting the wrong person.

Sunami drew aim on Mario's back just as he reached the limo. Mario scrambled into the limo while the unknown woman pumped slugs toward Sunami in an attempt to cover Mario.

Shadow raced from the Hummer and ran toward Sunami. Shadow dragged him backward toward the Hummer. When the woman dove back into the limo, Bullet slid across the hood of the blue Lincoln. He had to stop the limo from leaving.

As the limo pulled off, Bullet reached for the back door. The woman in the limo shot through the driver's side back window and shot Bullet in the face.

"Daddy!" Brianna yelled. The Cuban woman violently slapped Brianna across the face with a backhand.

Blood trickled from the corner of her mouth.

The limo raced from the parking lot and jumped the curve.

"Help, I've been shot!" Bullet screamed with both hands covering his face. "Fuck, I can't see!"

As everything slowly came back into realization, people yelled and screamed and scrambled in all directions.

Scar lifted Bullet across his shoulder and walked him over to the Humdeville.

Shadow looked across the lot at Brittany's lifeless body, wondering if taking her with them would be best.

"She's dead, Shadow, nothing you can do," said Hypnotic. "She's gone, now get out of there now!" she yelled, hoping he would understand.

"Swing around and pick me up, E-4," said Shadow.

"On my way!" Everlyn responded.

"O-5 and P-7, the limo is headed your way. Follow it, they still have Brianna!" Shadow yelled. "Don't lose her!"

Outlaw started the bike and pulled off. Shadow ran across the parking lot to the bodies of the Cubans. He pumped a slug into each one's head to make sure they were dead. "Now run tell that, bitch!"

Hypnotic packed her gun and wondered who the woman was. She knew that this woman would pose a serious threat if not stopped. She appeared to be dangerous, treacherous, and ruthless.

Keese

Chapter 15

For the next three hours, everyone sat in Sunami's living room and discussed the morning's events.

Hypnotic explained to them all that Brittany was murdered to send a message. Sunami didn't quite understand. Hypnotic explained that her murder was to prove that he would, in fact, kill the girl if he didn't return the money.

"Have you even seen that woman before, Shadow?" Hypnotic asked.

"Fuck no! And she better pray I never see her ass again in life. That's my word!"

"How did you make out on the photos?" Passion asked Hypnotic.

"I think I did okay. It's frustrating using that camera, but I got some good shots of everyone."

"Good," said Sunami.

"Now what?" Everlyn asked Hypnotic.

"Now we print the photos and show them around town to see if anyone can lead us to the men or tell us where they live. We might get lucky and find out where they're keeping Brianna."

"Sounds like a plan to me. Let's do it!" Bullet entered the room with his face scratched up and badly bruised.

Ms. Story glanced over at him. "What are you doing out of bed?"

"Scratcher don't stop a trooper. We got to find Sunami's daughter. So, let's do it! That's what the hell I'm here for."

"Yeah... but—" Shadow said as he stood to his feet.

"But nothing, nigga! That bitch tried to kill me, and somebody in them damn streets know them motherfuckers. All we gots to do is start shaking motherfuckers up in this town and somebody gonna start talking. Trust me!"

Hypnotic asked Sunami about the disk that Mario handed him.

"Oh shit!" he said and raced upstairs to retrieve the disk from his coat pocket. He came back downstairs, examined the disk, and realized that it was a DVD instead of a CD. He popped it into the DVD player and pressed play.

There was static, then a picture appeared on the screen. Shadow and Nickel Bag appeared on the screen. Both men had been recorded by a hidden camera in the closet.

"Do any of you know this guy Mellow?" Hypnotic asked. Everyone looked puzzled. She could tell that they didn't have a clue what she was thinking.

She held the disk for all to see. "In a court of law, this disk would be admitted as an admission to a crime. On the other hand, it's also information that could lead a good detective to a kidnapped child."

"How you figure that, I see nothing but incriminating evidence against us," Everlyn said.

"For example, Nickel Bag stated to Shadow that he was forced to hold drugs and money for this Mellow character, right?" said Hypnotic. Everyone agreed.

"Mellow's girlfriend is named Denise, right?" Sunami asked.

"Yeah, I know her very well. We used to date," said Shadow.

"That should be very helpful later," said Hypnotic.

Ms. Story cut in. "I don't understand. How's that gonna help us?"

"I'm getting to that in a moment," said Hypnotic.

"Some guy named Rock kidnapped Nickel Bag's little girl and her mother, right?"

Before she could speak another word, Sunami's eye met hers and for the first time, he found himself able to read her thoughts. "You're thinking that could be the same bastard that kidnapped Brianna and Brittany? But it can't be Rock. He was killed sometime last week in a robbery."

Bullet cut in. "What about that nigga Raw? That's their man and all. He could be next to step up in rank. Betcha that nigga know something."

"Who's this Raw fella?" Hypnotic asked. "And what could he have to do with all that's going on?"

"Raw a little short, ugly motherfucker," Bullet began while rolling a blunt. "Him, Mellow, and Rock were some Heckle and Jeckel type niggas. They were always together. Raw transported all the drugs for them clowns. Them niggas had the Southside on lock, so if you ask me, nigga got to know something."

Shadow cut in. "I know the bitch. Want me and Everlyn to bag his ass up?"

"Can you?" Hypnotic asked.

"Say no more! Consider it done."

Ms. Story made drinks for everyone. Hypnotic suggested that Raw, Denise, and her sister be found ASAP.

Her feeling was that whoever had Brianna had the original copy of the disk.

While deep in conversation, a car horn blew outside the front of the house. They all ran to the door and soon discovered that it was Hypnotic's brother. She opened the door and welcomed him in, as Shadow and Sunami helped him with his luggage.

"Why didn't you call first?" she asked while hugging him tightly. "We could've picked you up from the airport."

"I called you like six times this morning, but I got no answer."

"We were out this morning searching for Brianna. You do remember, don't you?"

"Any luck?" her brother asked, sensing the sadness in her eyes.

"I'm afraid not, but we're slowly making progress."

Sunami stood silently while desperately trying to remember where he'd seen this tall man before. His face was familiar. The guy could pass for Brian Mcknight.

"Man, you look familiar. Damn, you're the guy I saw Hypnotic leaving McDonald's with!" Sunami said.

"Douglas, this is Sunami, the guy I told you about," said Hypnotic.

After all the formal introductions, she brought her brother up to speed on what was going on and what had already taken place. He couldn't believe that she was running around with a bunch of street thugs, but he understood and couldn't wait to join them.

Keese

"Sis, you know we'll be breaking every law made by man." Douglas strapped on his shoulder holster. "So that means we can't leave anyone alive. Nobody! We don't want this shit coming back to bite us in the ass later, you feel me?"

"I don't think you have to worry about that with these guys," said Hypnotic.

Sunami cut it. "You ain't looking at nothing but killers. We done killed more niggas than Smith and Wesson, my nigga."

"How do you dispose of the bodies?" Douglas asked.

"Gangsters don't tell. If I tell you that, I'ma have to kill you."

"Cool. One thing, though."

"What's that, bro?"

"Why the hell we still standing around here? We got work to put in. Let's get busy!"

Chapter 16

Shadow and Everlyn observed all the drug activity on Enterprise Street from his Humdeville. He glanced at his Rolex and saw that the time was approaching 11 p.m.

Crackheads walked up and down the block in search of their next high.

A dark-skinned man who resembled Sticky Fingaz stood on the corner drinking Hennessey. Every so often, he would look around as though he was expecting someone to jump out at him. This guy passed something to the driver of an old beat-up Ford and seconds later, the car pulled off.

"Let's go do this," Shadow said, looking at Everlyn.

She slowly pulled from the curb, lowered the volume on the music, and pulled up and stopped in front of the guy.

"Yeah, what you need, ma?" the guy asked her.

"I need a dub. You ain't out yet, are you?"

The guy stared her down for a second. "Nice ride you got here. Is it yours?"

"Nah, it's my boyfriend's. He's at work right now. Why, you need a ride someplace?"

"Nah, I'm chillin'." He passed the crack through the window. Suddenly, his wrist was grabbed as Shadow pulled him halfway through the window. Everlyn sped off with squealing tires. A few blocks away, she stopped.

Two guys appeared from the darkness like thieves.

They grabbed the drug dealer, handcuffed him, and threw him into the back of the Hummer.

Before he could utter a word, the drug dealer was knocked unconscious by Douglas with his gun.

"Anybody see anything?" Sunami asked.

"Nah, I had you, my nigga," said Shadow.

"So, this that nigga Raw, huh?" Douglas asked.

"That's him," Shadow replied.

"I wonder what kind of information he can't wait to tell us?" Douglas asked, smiling.

Raw woke up twenty minutes later with a splitting headache. He thought he was blind, but soon realized he was indeed kidnapped and had no idea where the hell he was.

"You awake, my nigga?" an accented voice asked moments after he was dashed in the face with kerosene.

"Who that?" Raw asked.

"Your worst fucking nightmare."

Raw felt a hard, violent blow to the solarplex that knocked the breath out of him.

"We ask the damn questions around here. You do the answering," said Douglas.

"Fuck that! Let's body this bitch ass nigga," said Everlyn.

"If he doesn't talk, yeah, you can kill him." Douglas removed Raw's blindfold.

Raw lifted his head and stared down the barrel of a 380. He realized that he was about to be killed with his own gun and tears swelled in his eyes.

"Look at this pussy," said Shadow. "Never thought it could happen to you, huh?"

"I know who you are. You Sunami, ain't you?" Raw asked.

Sunami stepped forward and slapped Raw across the face with a gun. "You writing a damn book or something, motherfucker?!" He slapped him a second time.

"Told you we ask the damn questions here!"

"What you want, man? I don't get no beef with you."

"Who the fuck is Mario?" Sunami showed him the photo.

"Never seen him before."

Everlyn punched him in the jaw. "You lying bitch! That's the wrong answer! You and Mellow work for him, don't you?"

"I've never seen him before; I swear on my life!"

"Well, who do you work for?" Douglas asked.

"Two cops."

Sunami quickly looked at Douglas. "What fucking cops?"

"Officers Gazelle and Generette. I work for them, man. I don't know no Mario."

"Where these cops live?"

Hood Consigliere

"Don't know. I always beep them and they tell me where to meet them. They send their bodyguards to pick up their money from me and if they don't hear from me, they'll be out searching."

They beat and tortured Raw for another hour. When they were satisfied that they received all the information they needed, Everlyn grabbed the gas can and drenched the man. He thrashed about in the chair and tried to escape. She then lit a blunt and tossed it in his lap.

Raw hollered for dear life as his clothes ignited with hot flames. He bolted from the chair, slammed blindly into a wall, and fell to the floor, screaming for God's help.

"Now all of a sudden you a Christian?" Everlyn asked jokingly.

"Niggas kill me with that bullshit."

"Shit, at least the ropes burned and freed his ass," Douglas clowned.

"Look at that motherfucker. Sounds like a bitch watching a horror flick," said Shadow.

They could hear his hair and skin sizzling. Douglas grabbed a fire extinguisher and sprayed out the flames on Raw. Burned flesh hung from his body like burned rubber, as he continued to smoke. He was still alive and begging God for help.

"Stop crying, bitch!" said Everlyn, as she stomped on his face.

"Strap him down," said Douglas.

They chained the half-dead man to the cinder blocks, cut off one of his fingers, and stuffed it in a jewelry box. "Now what?" Everlyn asked.

"Dump his ass in the water. Fish got to eat too," said Sunami. They wrapped him in a rug, then put that rug in a plastic bag and loaded him in the back of a stolen truck.

"Shadow, you and Everlyn ditch this nigga and meet us at the house," Sunami ordered. "Me and Douglas gonna try and catch up with these two cops."

They all exited the abandoned building and headed in opposite directions. To them, the night was still young and there was much more work to be done.

"This thing got a phone?" Douglas asked as he looked around Sunami's Humdeville.

"Yeah, why? What's up?"

"This Gazelle and Generette... I'ma see if we can draw them out into the field. You know, pull them into our ball park."

"I feel ya, but how we gonna pull that off?"

"Simple! All we have to do is put the cheese on the tray. They'll come running, trust me."

"Aight. Where you gonna get this cheese?"

He glanced at Sunami with a devilish grin. "My sis and Everlyn. Sis will know just how to handle it, believe that!"

"I don't know about them two going against cops...we don't know nothing about these cats yet. They could be stone-cold killers."

"Stop worrying! My sis more dangerous than you think. Don't let them good looks fool you. Besides, you think I would suggest it if I thought she couldn't handle it? Shit, it's a walk in the park for her, right down her alley."

"She does have skills, and she's nasty with a rifle."

"Oh, you noticed, huh? You haven't seen shit yet, son."

Sunami spent the time talking about how much he admired Hypnotic's performance and skills.

Douglas was reading between the lines. He could tell that Sunami had a great deal of trust in his sister. He could also sense how much he liked her.

"You paid my sister's way down here?"

"No disrespect, duke, but your sister is all that. I had to put my bid in."

"Did you get the drawers yet?" Douglas asked with seriousness.

"Man, I'm not about to discuss our sex life with you! No sweat, though, cause if I had a sister, I'd probably be like you too. So, what's up with you, duke? Anybody special in your life?"

"Nah, not at the moment. I'm too busy in the streets working the beat. Man, we need to hit Hypnotic up and see how they coming along. They should be back at the house by now."

Sunami handed him the phone, he dialed the number and held the phone to his ear. "Hello," a voice whispered.

"What's good, sis?"

"You know, the job. How y'all making out? Everything okay? How's my man holding up?"

Douglas looked over at Sunami. He seemed very distant, as if he was in deep thought about his daughter.

"He's standing strong, sis.

"Lord, Douglas, I hope nothing happens to that little girl of his. She's done nothing to deserve this, not to mention she's already lost her mother."

"She'll be home soon."

Sunami slowed down at the corner of Chestnut Street and parked the Hummer. He got out with no warning to Douglas and slammed the door closed.

Douglas raced from the truck to catch up. "Sis, let me call you back. Something just came up."

Sunami walked between two parked cars, stepped on the sidewalk, and approached a gang of hoodlums playing CeeLo.

A short, brown-skinned guy with short hair turned to face him. Both men looked into each other's eyes like cowboys on the verge of drawing their guns in a western flick.

"Nigga, you a crazy motherfucker coming over here on my side of town," the guy said to Sunami. "Damn near every motherfucker on this side of town looking for your crazy ass. Nigga like me hear your ass is worth $95,000 balls, baby."

"And?" Sunami responded.

"I'm saying, you come out here like you bulletproof and shit. Just because you got those niggas on the South and Enterprise shook, don't mean you run shit here."

Sunami eyed all nine men standing out there, not giving a damn what they thought. He had one thing on his mind that he was ready to die for... his daughter.

Sunami stepped forward, only a breath away from the man's face, close enough to smell the Henny on his breath. "You pussy ass, panty-wearing bitch. If you or any one of your peoples even think about disrespecting my gangster, I'll come through Southside deeper than a gang of fucking Mexicans."

"Fuck you, bitch," someone yelled from the crowd.

"I don't give a fuck how many niggas they say you killed."

A young boy wearing a Durham Bulls hat, appearing to be no more than sixteen, stepped forward and flashed a 10mm tucked in his waistline.

Sunami stared into the kid's eyes, then pulled out a blunt, lit it, and pulled hard until his lungs were filled to capacity. Slowly exhaling, he said, "You know what I like about Southside, shorty? Y'all some simpleminded motherfuckers." He blew smoke straight into the kid's face.

The kid raised his hand to his face, and in that split second, Sunami snatched the boy's gun. He violently backhanded him with it and kicked the boy's feet from underneath him. The young thug fell hard to the ground.

Sunami thumbed the handle of the metallic one-eyed monster and aimed at the boy, point-blank range. The boy's eyes were wide with fear and he tried desperately to scoot back.

A murmur of confusion shot through the crowd like a shock wave. Everyone screamed at Sunami not to shoot the young kid. The young thug's eyes filled with tears and his vision blurred.

The kid was just a follower of what he never understood. Sunami couldn't hate him for that, but he couldn't allow this boy to just disrespect him either.

Sunami looked the wannabe thug square in the eyes and said, "Motherfucker, if you ever disrespect me again in life, I'll kill you without blinking! Never flash your gat if you're not willing to pull, shoot, and kill your enemy. And most of all, don't depend on your friends. They'll leave you hanging every time. Now get up!"

Once the kid stood to his feet, Sunami removed the clip from the gun, ejected the bullet from the breach, and tossed the gun on the pavement. He then grabbed the boy by the collar and lifted him to his toes. "Get your young ass off these streets. Ain't shit out here for you but death. Your mother is probably worried sick about you. I'm telling you some good shit!" He released the boy. "When you turn eighteen, come see me if I'm still living." Sunami smiled at the boy and handed him a wad of one-hundred-dollar bills. "And buy your mom something too."

Sunami stepped backward and looked all the gamblers in the face. "Yesterday, my daughter was kidnapped, and the first person who finds her or can tell me where she is, I'll give that person $10,000."

Everyone started mumbling. They couldn't believe their ears, but they know he spoke the truth. "How we gonna find you?" someone asked.

"Here's my cell phone number.'" He handed each one of them his personal black business card with white lettering. "It's always on. The other number is my man. Call either one of us, aight?"

"You for real, man?" someone asked.

"Do I look like I'm playing? Money is not an object. I'm for real, son."

Sunami and Douglas got back in the SUV and drove off. Douglas smiled while they listened to the radio.

"Whatcha smiling at, my nigga?"

"My sister said you was a crazy motherfucker. But I just found out how crazy you are."

"Sometimes, you got to do what's got to be done."

"You did the right thing, if you ask me. After a minute or two, I thought you were gonna need backup, but you handled it very well."

"Been doing this shit too long to be making mistakes, Doug." Silence passed by them for a moment as they waited at a stop light. Sunami smashed his half-size blunt out in the ashtray.

"Listen, man," said Douglas. "While you were roughing those boys, I called my sister back. We came up with a plan for those cops."

"Damn, I almost forgot about our office friends. Whatcha come with?"

Douglas explained everything that Hypnotic told him about their plan to kidnap the officers. Sunami thought it was a beautiful plan. Hypnotic was a brilliant strategist, and he admired that about her.

Keese

Chapter 17

Sunami and Shadow sat a short distance from Dunkin Doughnuts over by Bluefield. Douglas sat in the back looking through a pair of binoculars.

Shadow glanced at his watch to check the time. It read 1:30 p.m. "Man, we been following these bitches since ten this morning. We could have been took these faggots by now."

"Patience is a virtue when dealing with motherfuckers like them," Sunami responded.

"Heads up, y'all, they moving," said Douglas. "They leaving now!"

Both officers exited the Dunkin Doughnuts. Once outside, they climbed into their car and slowly pulled out into heavy traffic. At a distance, Sunami followed from behind as they headed west. No more than a mile down the road, they turned left at the light, and Sunami continued to follow them. Douglas reached for the phone and dialed a number.

As the large Hummer pulled into traffic, Hypnotic and Everlyn followed close behind in Shadow's BMW.

They got the call they'd been waiting on.

"Hello," Hypnotic said as she answered her cell phone.

"What's up, sis, how y'all?"

"We okay. How 'bout y'all?"

"We all good. You girls ready to proceed as planned?"

"Yeah," she said flatly.

"What's wrong? You sound a little nervous. You don't have to do this if you're not up to it."

"No! I'm fine, just a little tired. Sunami twisted and turned all night, so I didn't sleep very well."

"Would you like to speak with him before this all goes down?"

"Nah, I need to remain focused right now. Just give me the word when you're ready, okay?"

"Yeah."

"I'ma leave the phone on so you can hear everything."

"Aight! Whenever you ready, do your thing."

"We only nine cars behind y'all. Here I come now."

She looked over to Everlyn in the passenger's seat. Everlyn knew that look all too well. "Yeah, I'm ready. Just hope this plan of yours is official, girl."

"Trust me. I see no reason why it shouldn't work."

The BMW moved and handled the road very much to her liking. Hypnotic steered from left to right, cutting through traffic and passing cars. She was traveling at 100 mph, and knew she was breaking the law as she sped down the long highway.

She zigzagged around Sunami's Hummer and cut in front of him. The engine growled like a cat in heat as she closed in on the police car. She gripped the steering wheel tightly and turned with a short jerk. She curved around the cop car and accelerated faster. She looked down at the speedometer…110 mph.

She glanced in the rearview mirror and saw the cop car getting smaller by the second. In an instant, red and blue flashing lights came to life. She slowed the car down and pulled over.

"Aight, girl," she said to Everlyn as she checked her lipstick in the rearview mirror. "We only got one chance to do this right."

Both officers climbed slowly from the car and carefully approached the BMW with their hands on their side arms.

"What took you officers so long?" Hypnotic asked as she smiled flirtatiously. "Me and my cousin here thought you would never pull us over."

The officers were somewhat puzzled by her excitement. "Why would someone want to be ticketed for speeding?" Officer Gazell asked. "Excuse me, ma'am, but are you okay?"

She noticed his eyes conducting a visual search for open alcohol containers or drug paraphernalia.

"Sure, Officer. Me and my cousin was wondering if you two would like to have dinner with us tonight."

A faint smile came across the officer's face. He looked her up and down. "Did you just ask me out on a date tonight?"

Hypnotic giggled like a high school chick. The officer suddenly found himself excited by the size of her bouncing breasts. She raised her hand and toyed with her earring. "Sure did, Mr. Policeman. I hope I didn't do all this speeding for nothing, cause I thought you boys like it nice, hard, and fast. And that's a nice sized gun you have there too."

"Can you ladies excuse us for a minute?"

"Sure."

Both officers walked to the back of the car. She eyed them through the rearview mirror. Everlyn looked over at Hypnotic with uncertainty in her eyes.

"Girl, don't start that," said Hypnotic. "Them niggas horny as a bull. We got'em watch."

"Shhh!" said Everlyn. "They coming back."

"May I see your license and registration?" said the officer with seriousness.

"Sure!" she responded and reached into her purse.

"Does this mean no date tonight?"

"I'm afraid so, ma'am. We clocked you running 110 in a 60-mph zone. I'm gonna have to give you a ticket."

Hypnotic quietly passed the officer her undercover ID and the registration for the BMW. She looked at the officer with sadness in her eyes.

"Here you are, ma'am. You both have a nice day."

The officer handed the ID and registration back to her, along with the ticket.

Something isn't right, Hypnotic thought to herself. She looked the ticket over and smiled as the officers got back into their car.

"Whatcha smiling at, girl?"

Hypnotic tossed the folded paper in her lap. She opened it and screamed.

"What's all the screaming, baby?" Sunami asked through the speaker phone.

"We did it, baby! He gave us his phone number and said to call at 6:30!"

"I knew you could pull it off."

"Shit, I was nervous as hell though," said Everlyn.

"So, how we gonna do this tonight? Cause them niggas wanna fuck," Hypnotic said. "We gonna need a place to take them."

Keese

"Listen, we're right behind y'all. Pull over up ahead at that gas station.

"We'll talk there," said Sunami. "I got just the place."

Chapter 18

After carefully developing a methodical plan, Sunami, Hypnotic, and Everlyn called the officers. They suggested to both that a nice, quiet meal at home with a little wine would be best. Officer Gazell agreed and provided them with an address and time for their get together.

"Okay, we're set to meet them at 8:30," Hypnotic nervously said to her brother.

"So far so good," said Douglas. "So, they didn't mind you calling back to reschedule the time?"

"Not at all," she said, looking at Sunami.

Something was bothering her, Sunami could tell. Something about the situation didn't feel right to him either.

He asked Hypnotic to speak with him in private. They excused themselves from the living room. "Baby, listen," he began while looking into her eyes. "Everything you have done for me thus far has been more than enough. If you not feeling this plan, it won't change nothing if you back down. We'll still be cool."

She thought about it for a moment. She turned slowly, walked over to the bed, and sat down. She looked at Sunami. "Come here," she said as she patted the bed.

"What's wrong? You aight?" He walked across the room and sat beside her.

She turned her face away from him in an attempt to hide her tears. Sunami placed a finger on the small of her chin and gently turned her face to his. He looked into her eyes and asked her again what was wrong.

"Six years ago, me and my partner conducted an undercover sting. I had to pretend to be this cop's lover so I could gather inside information on him and his drug operation. My partner was a female and dating this cop's brother. On the night we were supposed to take them down, the house was stormed by police. I drew my weapon and ordered him to get down on the floor. He refused to listen and attacked me. I shot him in the chest. He continued to struggle, and I heard my partner calling for help, but I couldn't get free. When I finally did get away, I searched the house with back-up. We found my partner dead. She had been shot in the head from behind. She never had a chance to draw her weapon."

Sunami took her in his arms with a caring embrace.

"I promise you, beautiful, I won't let anything happen to you."

She pulled away. "It's not you or me I'm worried about. It's Everlyn. The moment we walk into that cop's house, her life will be in my hands. It's like déjà vu for me."

"That was a long time ago, and I think what you're doing is a good thing. I don't know too many people willing to keep it real like you."

"Sunami, you don't understand. I have your daughter's and Everlyn's lives in my hands."

"Come here," he said with open arms. "Everything will be okay. These people we're about to go up against have no idea who they're fucking with right now. But like I said, if you don't want to go through with it, we can try to figure something else out."

She kissed him passionately on the lips. It was a long, slow, intense kiss. She then stopped abruptly. "I want to do this. Brianna needs our help more than ever."

"You sure?"

"Umm hmm," she mumbled. "I know you don't make promises, but can you make another?"

"Another? What promise did I already make?"

"You promised to let nothing happen to me. Now I want you to promise that you'll let the game go and raise your daughter once we get her back. Put all this behind you."

"I promise!" Sunami checked the time. "It's about that time. You ready?"

She nodded yes and kissed him lightly on the lips.

They spent a few moments going over their plan.

Both women carried concealed weapons. Both women were nervous but felt the risk they were about to take was well worth it.

When they reached the officer's house, they parked three houses down to remain on the safe side. Both women got out of the car, walked down the sidewalk, and noticed three cars parked in single file. They reached the house and climbed the stairs. Hypnotic reached into her purse and pressed send on her cell phone, sending Sunami a signal that they were at the right house.

When she saw Passion step out to check her tire, she shut the phone off. "You ready, Everlyn?"

"Let's just do this and get it over with."

Hypnotic knocked on the door. After the third knock, an average-sized man answered the door. "Hope we're not too late, we drove as fast as we could," she said and smiled.

"Oh no! Please do come in."

Both women stepped into the house. Everlyn looked around and took notice of things just as Hypnotic told her to do. The house was cozy and comfortable. She could tell by the furniture that the officer was once married. The house smelled of stale tobacco.

"Let me help you with your coat." The cop stepped behind Hypnotic and then Everlyn, and helped each woman remove her coat.

He suggested they both have a seat on the sofa. He grabbed his television remote, turned on the television, and handed it to Hypnotic.

"Thank you, Gazelle," she said to show politeness.

"Please, last names are not necessary between us. Call me Kevin. My partner will be down in a minute."

"Well, well. Good evening, ladies." The second cop's voice suddenly filled the room. "Have any problems finding the house?"

"None whatsoever. You look nice tonight. You seeing someone behind by back?" Everlyn asked jokingly.

"What, are you joking me? I would never." He smiled and sat beside her. "My name is Nick, and you are?"

"Call me Everlyn."

"Excuse me, Kevin, can we use your bathroom?" Hypnotic asked.

"Sure, go right ahead. It's at the top of the stairs to the right. Can't miss it."

Both women went up the stairs and into the bathroom. Hypnotic closed the toilet and sat on it. Everlyn took a deep breath and sat on the side of the tub. Both women reached into their purses, pulled out leather gloves, put them on, and then pulled out their 9 mm Brownings.

Both guns were equipped with silencers.

"You ready?" Hypnotic asked as she stood to her feet.

Everlyn looked nervous, but ready. "Yeah, let's get this shit over with." She used a rag she found on the sink to wipe down everything they touched, including the doorknob.

Hypnotic opened the door, stuck her head out to look around, and then quietly motioned to Everlyn to follow behind her. They walked down the steps like skillful assassins creeping in the dark.

Both men were sitting on the sofa, drinking beer and watching the latest sports highlights. The women hid the guns behind their backs.

Hypnotic stepped in front of the television. "Okay, boys, do y'all want to watch us heat it up in here, or watch them boys in loose shorts play with balls?"

The men looked at each other with shit-eating grins on their faces and turned their attention back to the women.

The women quickly drew their guns. The men flinched and desperately tried to grab their backup weapons strapped to their ankles.

Hypnotic squeezed her trigger and shot at one man's kneecap, which exploded into grisly particles of blood and bone. A second later, her gun jumped again, hitting the second cop's kneecap. Both men screamed in agony.

"Bitch, shut your fucking fat face before I splatter your ear, you piece of shit!" Hypnotic yelled. "Those shots were to show you I know how to aim."

"Fuck you, you cunt," Officer Generette cursed.

Hypnotic shot again, this time blowing off small bits of his ear. "Guess you didn't hear me, huh? Bet your ass hear me now."

The officer grabbed what was left of his ear. Blood oozed through the cracks of his fingers.

Okay, lady, please! No more shooting," said a terrified Gazelle. "I'll tell you where the money is. Just don't kill me."

"Everlyn, open the back door. I'll handle them,"

140

Hypnotic ordered. "You both need to listen to me very carefully now. All you have to is answer some questions. If you do that, you might make it out alive."

"Alive my ass, I'm killing both these pigs!" Sunami spat as he and the others entered the house. "Bitches gonna tell me what I wanna know one way or another!"

They cuffed both men and bound their legs together with the speed of a cowboy at a rodeo show, as Shadow and Douglas prepared to go to work. They then dragged both men across the floor into the kitchen, feet first. Sunami and Douglas sat both men in chairs.

"Do you, ma!" Outlaw said to Everlyn. She stepped forward and violently punched Gazelle in the jaw with a pair of brass knuckles. The man hollered in pain, spitting blood from his mouth.

"My name is Sunami. All you motherfuckers at the station know me, and been trying to bring me down for a minute. So, you know how I get down. So, this is how it's gonna be. You tell me exactly what I need to know, then me and my people will be outta here. Simple as that."

Officer Gazelle's head rolled back. "I don't give a rat's ass who you are. You're a low life piece of shit, if you ask me. So, fuck you, cause we ain't telling shit. Cops don't snitch."

Sunami slapped him across the face with his gun.

"It's you fucking niggas who's always good for ratting each other out. Fuck you!" Sunami stepped back and asked the cop if he knew Mario.

The officer refused to answer. Sunami ordered Shadow to pull out a pair of pliers. He slowly repeated the question. When the cop said 'fuck you,' Sunami looked at Shadow and nodded his head in silence.

Shadow kneeled down and with Douglas's help, removed the cop's shoes and socks. Douglas held the cop's left foot as he thrashed about in his seat and yelled.

Sunami ordered Outlaw to muffle the pig by stuffing a dish rag into his mouth. Once he was silenced, Shadow used the pliers to ruthlessly snatch the cop's big toenail off. Crimson red blood squirted from the exposed would.

Passion dashed across the room and grabbed a box of salt. She poured it over the cop's big toe. The cop hollered wildly, as the rag almost gagged him. Tears filled his eyes and sweat covered his face. Sunami snatched the cloth from his mouth and asked him if he felt like cooperating now.

The officer was breathing heavily. "Fuck you!" he yelled.

"Motherfucker, you tough, huh? You so tough you willing to die for anything. I'ma see how tough you are when I have shorty cut off that little dick of yours and stuff it in your mouth!"

Everyone in the room looked at Sunami. They all thought and felt the same way. Sunami was getting beside himself. He had a crazy look in his eyes that none of them had ever seen before.

"What?" Sunami yelled at everyone. "This motherfucker probably knows exactly where my daughter is. I don't give a fuck about this nigga! We came over here to handle one thing, and I'm about to handle this shit! Y'all can look at me crazy if you want to! Fuck both these bitches. They gonna talk!"

Sunami held a knife he'd taken from the kitchen drawer to the man's ear. He then chopped it loose from his head. Blood oozed profusely from his head, and the cop tried to escape his seat in desperation.

Sunami pushed him back to his seat and looked over at the other cop, who was forced to watch his partner got through this ordeal. He then turned his attention back to Gazelle.

"Passion, pull this faggot's pants down and cut off his dick!" shouted Sunami. Passion stared at Sunami for a moment. She was afraid of what might happen to her if she didn't comply.

She accepted the knife from Sunami and cut the cop's pants to allow access to his groin. Once she had his member in her hand, she turned her head and swiftly severed his penis from his body.

When Gazelle saw her holding his unattached member, he mumbled through clenched teeth.

"Oh, now you wanna talk!" said Shadow. "Fuck that, it's too late! Bullet, kill that bitch!" Bullet pulled his gun from his waist and shot the bastard in the head.

The officer slumped down, resting his chin on his chest. He was dead.

An extremely frightened Generette mumbled through the rag stuffed in his mouth. Sunami walked over and snatched the rag from his mouth.

"Something you want to tell me, Mr. Policeman?"

"Please, please…just don't kill me. I'll tell you anything."

"Now that just might save your life," Sunami said with coldness in his voice.

"If I tell you what you want, will you let me be?"

"If I let you be, will you come after us?"

The cop swore he would keep his mouth shut.

However, Sunami knew he was lying. He'd never met an honest cop in his life.

"Who's this, Mario? He has my daughter."

The cop's eyes moved wildly. "My partner and I met him about eight years ago. His brother is Cuba…if anybody has your daughter, it might be him."

The cop took a deep breath. "Mario and Cuba came here eight years ago. Cuba's wife was trafficking some pure, uncut cocaine back and forth from up north, until one day a trooper pulled her over. She's a killer too, cold blooded! When the young trooper walked over to her window, she put two bullets in his face, point blank. She then sped down 95 and ran into a roadblock. She was surrounded but refused to give up. She peeled out in reverse and hit about three or four of our guys."

"What happened to this woman?" Hypnotic asked.

"She's pulling life in the feds."

"So, who the fuck is the bitch Mario got at his side now?" said Sunami.

The cop shrugged his shoulders. "Can't really say."

Hypnotic slapped him. "Try to say!"

The cop coughed before speaking. "Her name is Amil. She's half Haitian and Cuban. Watch her. She's Cuba's daughter and personal hit man."

"Something don't add up. Why would Cuba have Brianna and Brittany kidnapped and not Sunami? This doesn't make sense," said Hypnotic.

"Well, Cuba didn't know what Sunami looked like. So, he calls me one night and tells me he needs somebody black from the south side for some kidnapping work. Me and my partner spike with these E-Jay and Omega characters, guys with rap sheets as long as my arm."

Suddenly, Sunami's face twisted out of shape and turned beet red with anger.

"You know them?" Douglas asked.

Sunami was silent for a moment. "I'ma kill them. Ain't nothing to talk about when I see them!"

The kitchen was graveyard silent. Only the loud ticking of the clock on the wall could be heard.

"So did E-Jay and Omega do the kidnapping themselves?" Hypnotic asked. The cop nodded his head yes.

"Do these two have her now?"

"I don't know," the cop replied. "Cuba never spoke of it afterward. But if I had to guess, I'd say he has her."

"If Cuba don't know me, then how the hell he find my daughter and her mother?" Sunami asked.

"The bank teller downtown gave us your daughter's mother's address. Mellow told us she knew her because she comes into the bank every Friday to cash her check. Cuba paid her $15,000 for the address."

"Where does Cuba live? You got his address?"

The cop gave them Cuba's address and phone number. Sunami leveled his gun and shot the cop in the face, killing him instantly. "Somebody cut that nigga's head off," he whispered. "We're gonna send Mario, Cuba, and that bitch Amil a little message."

"And the bitch Denise, I'ma kill her. She done fucked up," Shadow swore.

"Nah, baby, let me and Passion put that work in on her," Everlyn said. Shadow nodded his head in silence as he turned and walked away.

Hypnotic reminded them that the cops offered her money and that they should search the house for it before they cleaned up and bounced.

Keese

Chapter 19

Sunami and the others spent all day Thursday searching Durham for Omega and E-Jay, only to turn up short. They discovered that both men were out of town.

Sunami was extremely irritated and felt like he spent the day on a wild goose chase. He was getting more and more worried about his only child, and tried desperately to push all negative thoughts from his mind.

Early Friday morning, Hypnotic cooked scrambled eggs, pancakes, bacon, and hash browns for him.

"Sunami, baby, take a long hot shower. You'll feel much better. You've been wearing those clothes since yesterday."

He smiled at her and for a few seconds, her beauty distracted his thoughts from the troubling situation. He went upstairs, undressed, and entered the shower as if he could wash away his past.

He dried off, climbed back in bed, and fell asleep.

An hour later, the phone rang. It was the call he'd been waiting for since six o'clock the night before. He was startled and stared at the phone, which was his private line for business only.

He picked up the phone. "Yo! What's good?"

"It's me," the caller said. "Them niggas just stepped into the house, man!"

Sunami slung around and put his feet on the floor.

"Is everybody in position like they supposed to be?"

"No question! To the fullest! You want me to bag this nigga for you?"

"Nah, this one's personal, dawg. If he leaves, I want a five-man tail on his ass at all times."

"No sweat, my nigga."

"What about them two bitches?" Sunami asked. "You got someone on them too?"

"Yeah, but for now, they still at work. I'm handling it though."

"Aight, anything else, my nigga?"

"Not right now, dawg... Something just came up, I'll let you know."

"Aight, just hit me on my cell. I'm about to get up and head out there. Damn! It's 1:30 already. I must have been tired."

"Yeah!"

"I'ma holla!"

Sunami hung up the phone, dressed in black fatigues and a matching coat. He opened the closet and grabbed some smoke grenade canisters in case he needed them.

"You feeling better?" Hypnotic asked as he stepped into the living room. "You look much better. Damn, you going to war?"

He didn't answer. He walked across the room toward her and kissed her gently on the lips.

"Where you off to now?"

"E-Jay and Omega back in town. I'ma handle their asses."

"Would you like me to tag along?"

Sunami thought about what was about to take place.

"Nah, baby. These two guys are crazy as hell. When they laid their hands on my daughter, they signed their own death warrants. Hypnotic, it's not gonna be easy to kill these fools. And besides, it's probably gonna be an all-out street war. I don't want to risk you getting caught up in the middle of this shit."

"You will be coming back to me, right?" she asked in a trembling voice.

"You damn right, I'm coming back to you!"

"If you need me, don't hesitate to call."

"Aight. Be back later. I'm about to put these niggas on the front page." As he walked out the front door, Hypnotic called his name and he turned to face her.

"Put this on," she advised and handed him a bulletproof vest.

"I'm alright. I hate rocking those things. Besides, them niggas have no idea who I am and the team I command."

She stared at him in silence. Her look said, *I'm telling you, not asking, damnit.* "Damn, I hate it when you look at me like that, woman!" he mumbled, accepting the vest.

She smiled. "You got your gun? I don't see it," she said bluntly.

"It's out in the car. Besides, your brother and them got the shit I'ma need in the back of the Hummer."

"Please be careful and cover your ass."

He assured her he would. He also told her Everlyn and Passion would be handling Denise on his command, and that he needed her for tomorrow. She responded by telling him that she and Ms. Story would be visiting Cuba and Mario's estate to devise a plan for tomorrow night's attack.

He felt she was well suited for the job, and he trusted that she knew what she was doing. He would talk with her about it when he returned later.

When he left, he drove in silence to collect his thoughts. Mario told him he had until Sunday morning to return the money or his daughter was dead, and that thought lingered in his head the whole drive to Southside.

He fought the desire to call the man. He cursed under his breath because he knew such a call would only warn the man that he was coming. He prayed that Hypnotic knew what she was doing and that things went smoothly to get Brianna out of there safely.

Regardless, he had to trust her and his instinct. The woman was smart and cunning, and she had become his better half. He cleared and calmed his mind for the task at hand and smoked a blunt.

He was a block away from Omega's house. He pulled out his cell phone and dialed a number.

"Yo!" Shadow said.

"This me. I'm around the corner parking now. Come holla," Sunami said and ended the call. Moments later, Shadow arrived. Shadow brought Sunami up to speed on the situation. He explained how he had the house and windows completely surrounded, and all weaponry was ready.

Sunami simply said, "Ain't nothing more to talk about. Let's do it!" He suited up in his gear. He stopped to speak with his young bosses, captains, soldiers, and his known associates. The entourage of assassins were all from the Westside and part of his elite underworld task force team, know as Heavy Infantry.

No one in the city knew their identity, because they always covered their faces with masks. Everyone in town feared them, for they knew they meant business whenever they showed up.

"Weapons check!" Shadow yelled to the twenty men who stood by dressed in black fatigues with triple-threat level 3 bulletproof vests and black riot helmets with shatter-proof face shields, with microphones to allow communications.

They had semi-automatic pistols holstered on their hips, and around their waists were dump pouches holding spare magazines of ammunition. They looked more like a SWAT team. They were the best assassin's money could buy in Durham.

"Weapons ready and loaded," all men yelled in a unified order like troops standing before a commanding officer.

"Let 'em have it now!" Shadow yelled. Gunshots exploded like a chain of thunder. The men trembled and jerked as they held down the triggers of their weapons.

Shells ejected, flipped in the air, and pinged on the pavement.

Windows on the house shattered into small fragments, and wood chips exploded from the side, leaving golf-ball-size holes. A hail of bullets zipped through the air, forcefully penetrating anything in their path. The house now looked as if it had been shredded.

Screams from women and children nearby enveloped the air, and men stopped to reload. Ruffled feathers shouted at the men as sensitive car alarms blared loudly. Seconds later, the shooting continued. A strong, unpleasant smell of smoke filled the air.

The men stood in silence. Shadow examined their work. The house was completely shot up with holes. There was no way that anyone could have survived if they were inside. "Time to move out!" Shadow said as he turned to leave.

Sunami grabbed Shadow's wrist. He knew it wasn't his call, and knew that he needed to confirm the man's death in order to be at peace. "Nah, we're going in. Everybody else take position and cover us!"

Sunami kicked the front door and entered M-16 first. They quickly searched the living room and found none of their enemies. They checked the kitchen, bedrooms, bathrooms, and closets. The house was completely empty.

"Motherfucker! I thought you said you seen them niggas come here!" Sunami screamed.

"Bullshit, I saw that nigga park, get out, and come in myself!" Shadow yelled back.

"Me too!" someone said from outside through the communication devices.

"Shit, we checked the whole house! If them niggas were in here, they'd be dead, all them bullets we pumped in this motherfucker!" Sunami said.

"Man, y'all got to get outta there. Cops about to come. I just heard it over the scanner," a voice said through the helmet.

"You know what to do if they show," Shadow said.

"Them niggas had to leave the house out the back door while we were talking down the block," Sunami said as he looked around. He went back to the living room and noticed that the sofa was out of place. He walked toward the sofa and noticed small drops of blood on the floor and smeared blood on the wall behind it. "Shadow, over here," he whispered, "I think them niggas is under us."

Sunami kneeled behind the sofa and touched the rug. He felt an uneven hump. Some kind of handle hadn't been fully closed. "Oh shit!" yelled Shadow as Sunami pulled open the trap door. Both of them looked and noticed a wooden ladder leading downward. Shadow told Sunami to back up and stuck his gun in first. He held the trigger and shot wildly until it was empty.

Sunami climbed down. The room was pitch black, so dark he couldn't even see his hand before his face. He and Shadow separated and moved in the dark like commandos in the deep jungle. "Ump!" Sunami grunted as he stumbled over something.

"You aight?" Shadow whispered.

"Yeah. See if you can find a light switch. It's dark as hell in here!"

Without warning, a staccato sound of gunshots rang out. Bright flashes in the dark created a strobe effect.

Shadow and Sunami dove to the floor and scrambled for cover. Shadow returned fire, aiming in the direction of the gun flashes.

"Ump," someone yelled and crashed to the floor.

"E-Jay!" yelled Omega, revealing his position by voice.

"You motherfuckers gonna have to kill me!" Omega moved into the room on the ball of his feet to minimize sound. He moved along the wall toward the light switch. He heard a faint sound but couldn't tell its direction. His heart thumped loudly in his ears. His breath was steady and heavy. He recalled a trick he once used when he was small.

He dug into his pocket for a cigarette lighter.

"Bitch, face the music! You fucking with the wrong family!" Sunami yelled out in the dark. "You know how I get down."

"Fuck that shit! Can't kill what you don't see," Omega yelled back.

Sunami wanted to shower the room with a hail of bullets but didn't want to take the chance of hitting Shadow. A small explosion went off in the room. The flash lit up the entire room for a second. Omega saw both men positioned on the other side of the room, directly before him.

Sunami realized that Omega had just tossed a light against the wall in order to use its explosion to see.

He told Shadow to hit the floor.

A second later, an Uzi roared angrily and sprayed shots throughout the room. "Oomph," Sunami yelled loudly. "Shadow, I'm hit. Can't feel my legs!"

The sound of a large weapon clattered to the floor.

The men outside informed Shadow that the cops were on their way and they needed to get out of there. Shadow yelled back that he needed more time. His men swore they would fight to the death for him. "Sunami! Hold on, bro. I'ma get you," Shadow yelled.

"Damn," Shadow said as he realized that someone had just flicked on the lights in the room. He stood less than twenty feet away from Omega. He looked around, noticed Sunami lying motionless and face down.

"Game over, nigga!" Omega laughed, pointing his gun at his target.

Shadow looked around, knowing he had nowhere to go. "Suck my dick, nigga!" Shadow yelled.

Click, click, click was the only sound heard as Omega pulled his trigger and discovered that his gun was empty. "Shit!" he cursed as he pulled out the clip.

Sunami stood quickly to his feet. "Bulletproof vest, my nigga!" he said as he raised his M-16. "Played dead, damn shame you can't play."

"It takes a coward to shoot a man with no gun," Omega yelled as he tossed his clip.

"Who said I was gonna shoot you? Shadow, no matter what happens, don't get in this. I owe this nigga. You don't fuck with my daughter. It's me and him."

Shadow nodded his head in agreement as Sunami passed him his gun. Suddenly, Omega charged Sunami as Shadow stepped back. They crashed to the floor. Sunami kneed Omega in the side and then elbowed him in the face. He then tossed Omega off of him. Sunami smashed his right fist into Omega's jaw, then his left. Blood oozed from Omega's mouth.

"I'ma kill you, motherfucker!" Sunami grunted.

Omega grabbed Sunami's wrist in a death-locking clutch and jabbed him in the face, snapping his head back as they both rolled in the dirt. Sunami then pulled a double-edged knife from his holster and slammed it straight into Omega's heart.

Sunami grunted while yanking the knife around, digging deeply into his chest. Omega stiffened as his eyes slowly rolled back in his head. He was dead, never even having the chance to grunt or yell. "Let's get the fuck out of here," Sunami said as he stood to his feet.

"Right behind you, my nigga," said Shadow as he passed him the M-16.

Both men shot E-Jay and Omega in the head to ensure their death and quickly scrambled up the ladder. As they exited the basement, Shadow informed Sunami that three cop cars had shown up and six cops were outside.

When the two men reached the front door, they readied their weapons as massive gunfire rang out in the streets.

Both men charged out into the yard and were joined by the other men who were desperately trying to kill the cops who had taken cover behind their vehicles. They were outnumbered eighteen to six, so they had no problem holding the police at bay.

The scene was chaotic confusion. Bullets bounced and ricocheted everywhere. The officers tried to take clear shots at the men all dressed in black.

Heavy Infantry was armed and ready, no matter what the consequences might be. "Damn! Y'all get the fuck out of here. I got 'em," Shadow ordered. He and Sunami were the only two with grenade launchers attached to their M-16s.

"Fade out!" Sunami yelled, ordering everyone to stand down. "Me and the point man will cover y'all."

The cops were using the protection of their car doors for cover as they returned fire. Bullets hissed in the air and passed Shadow's and Sunami's heads by inches. The men returned fire on the cops, disregarding earlier orders to fall back. Sunami repeated the order a second time, as SWAT and extra cops sped down the block toward them. They all scattered, leaving Sunami and Shadow behind.

Sunami dove to the ground, raised up on both his elbows, and then raised his weapon and aimed using his sight and pulled back on the trigger until his thirty-round clip was empty. He snatched the clip out and rolled over to his left as large chunks of earth exploded near his body. He slammed another clip in with his palm. He raised his gun and unleashed his full clip toward the cops.

Just as a cop peeked over the top of his car door, a bullet slammed right into his face, blowing his head apart. A second cop had crouched down on one knee by the car's front fender to reload his gun when a slug caught him in the nose and exploded through the back of his head.

As a professional stick-up artist and killer, Shadow adhered to one code. Kill or be killed. He could not allow the SWAT to exit that truck. "Sunami, cover me!" he yelled as he scrambled to his feet and ran toward the street.

Heavy gunfire showered his way. He sprinted zig zag and crashed back first into a car. He kept his head low and raced out into the street, diving into the air and turning sideways as he glided and spit fifteen rounds into the grill of the van. "Shit, I missed," he cursed.

He rolled to one knee, crouched low, and then thought about the words his paid instructor once told him... *I want you to get used to placing your shots exactly where you want them, because precision is the key in urban warfare.* Shadow knew that now was the time to produce.

He aimed his M-16 and fired a grenade through the window of the van with ice-pick accuracy.

A crackle followed by a loud explosion thundered.

Red and orange flames rose wildly from the van. The other cops were in shock and awe at what had just taken place and were totally unprepared for this situation.

"Ghost attack!" Sunami yelled to Shadow through the communication device. Sunami pulled smoke grenades from his belt and pulled the pins from them and tossed them in all directions. Within seconds, a heavy smoke cloud filled the air and reduced visibility.

As the smoke cleared, cops searched frantically for the gunmen who had suddenly vanished. Dead bodies of cops littered the streets. The scene was grisly.

"Damn, those sons of bitches were pretty damn bold," one cop cursed. The screams of little children, women, yelling fathers, and car alarms could be heard up and down the street.

Keese

Chapter 20

It was payday, and the bank was very busy. As closing time neared, Denise shut down her window. "See you Monday, Denise," said one of the other bank tellers as she walked by to leave.

"Okay, Adell. Tell the kids I said hello," she responded.

Denise then walked over to Kasara, who was seated at a desk. "You 'bout ready, girl? I know I'm ready to get out of here. My head is killing me like crazy."

"I know what you mean. Thank God it's Friday," Kasara responded. "You hear about the shooting today?"

"No, what shooting?"

"Lisa called about an hour ago and said the Heavy Infantry niggas shot up Omega and E-Jay's house."

"Girl, you playing!"

"Kid you not!" Kasara responded as they walked out the door to the parking lot. "Said police and all come out there, and them niggas shot 'em up gangster style."

"Kasara, something ain't right. Something is going on."

"Like what?"

"Rock got killed, then Nickel Bag, then Mellow. Then two cops, and now you saying they shot up Omega's house?"

"Why do you find that strange?" Kasara asked as she started the car. "Drug dealers and stick-up kids dying in Durham ain't new."

"Yeah, but think about it. They all from this side of town. And the police still haven't found Raw yet."

"Girl, Raw not trying to be found, if you ask me."

Kasara could tell something was really bothering her sister. As they drove home, Denise told her how she was responsible for Mellow getting robbed, which led to Rock's death. She also told Kasara that she had sold Sunami's daughter and her mother out and that her mother had been killed behind a drug beef. She said Sunami and Shadow were the ones responsible for all the recent murders.

Kasara could not believe what she was hearing. She stopped the car and cursed, as tears ran down her pretty face.

"Kasara, I'm so sorry. I didn't know how to tell you. I love you, sis."

"Get out!!!"

Denise didn't want to get out of the car, but realized she was around the corner from her house. She tearfully exited the car and closed the door. Kasara sped off and left her alone.

As she walked the block home, she heard the slam of a car door behind her. She looked around and saw Kasara walking toward the house.

They both sat silently on the front porch. Neither woman noticed the car parked across the street. "How long you gonna stay mad with me?" Denise asked with sadness in her eyes.

"Why, Denise?"

"Shadow promised me that nobody would be hurt. We were gonna split the money. Then this man comes along talking 'bout how he knows I used to date Shadow and that I had something to do with Mellow getting robbed. And for the life of me, I don't know how he found out."

"Is that the same guy who wanted Sunami's baby mama's address?"

"Yeah, he told me it was the only way to correct what I'd done. Then he gave me money to keep my mouth shut about it."

Kasara lifted her head and studied her sister's face for a moment. She tried to will herself to understand, but she just felt confused and betrayed. "But why him, Denise? He was the only guy I ever truly loved."

"I love you, and never meant to hurt you, Kasara. I hope you forgive me."

Their conversation was interrupted by the phone ringing inside the house. "I'll get it," said Denise. As she went to answer the phone, Kasara sat in silence awaiting her return.

A short distance across the street, Everlyn and Passion were sitting in a stolen Maxima smoking weed and sharing their intimate secrets.

"So, what made you come to North Carolina? Ain't New York better?" Passion asked between pulls of the blunt. "Ain't jack going on down here."

"Well, I haven't really moved down here, not yet anyway. My girlfriend Candy used to fuck Shadow, but then she got killed. He brought me down here."

"You like him?"

"Uh, yeah. But really, I'm after something else. You know how us girls are. Got to do what we got to do before the pussy ain't worth shit."

"How much you gonna take him for?" Passion asked. "Got mine. I'm playing the hell out of Bullet. First, I fake a pregnancy, then a miscarriage. Now he thinks we lost a child together."

"Girl, you good. You try that shit on them niggas in New York and those fuckers want to see paperwork and all. That's why I'ma get Shadow. I want half of everything."

"How the hell you gonna do that?"

"Hook him, bag him, marry him, then divorce him! Watch me. I done killed a motherfucker for him too. I hope he don't think I'm doing all this shit for nothing, cause he ain't all that!"

"You shoulda went after Sunami," said Passion.

Everlyn looked at the woman as if she was crazy as hell. "You seven thirty for real! That nigga straight gangsta. Besides, Hypnotic wants him."

"You think she gaming him?"

"Nah, she's a loyal motherfucker. She used to be down with some clique in Brooklyn, then she became a cop, but she's not one now. But on the real, I think she's keeping it real. That bitch ain't scared of shit. She told Sunami last night that she was gonna get his little girl back, even if it kills her. Now it doesn't get no realer than that."

Suddenly Passion jumped. "Look, look! That bitch's sister just went in the house. Let's murk that stank ass hoe right now." Both women got out of the car and walked across the street.

"Lift your head up, bitch! It's a good day to die!" Everlyn yelled.

Kasara raised her head and looked the two women square in their faces. She suddenly realized that they were wearing black leather gloves and had guns in their hands. Her first thought was to take off running, but her legs just wouldn't move.

"Bitch, next time you sell someone's address, you'll be doing it from hell!" Everlyn said and then pulled the trigger of the 9mm. The hollow-point bullets tore into the chest of Denise's identical twin.

When Denise heard the gunshot, she reached into her purse for her gun and then rushed toward door. She screamed when she saw her sister's body in a pool of blood.

Without hesitation, she aimed her 44 caliber 431 Special Taurus. As the barrel exploded with a thunderous boom, she noticed that her first shot hit its target dead center in the back and blood spurted from the hole in the woman's shirt.

Denise aimed and fired a second shot, and the impact of the slug lifted her second target and slammed her against the side of a car.

Denise dropped the gun, kneeled down beside her sister's body, and cried. Her crying turned to screaming as she realized her sister would never wake up again.

She laid Kasara's head to the ground and smoothed out her clothes. Denise stood to her feet, placed the barrel of her gun to her temple, and pulled the trigger, ending her own life instantly.

Chapter 21

Moments after leaving Cuba's estate, Hypnotic discovered she was being followed by a black Yukon. Ms. Story was sitting quietly in the passenger's seat and suggested they stop at this store just off Chapel Hill Road.

As Hypnotic made a right-hand turn, the Yukon continued to follow. They were now sure that the SUV was following them.

"Betcha somebody saw us taking pictures back there," said Ms. Story.

Hypnotic glanced her way. "You might be right about that, but why are they following us? They sure as hell ain't getting the camera."

She drove into the store's parking lot. The Yukon continued on its way. "You think we being paranoid?" Hypnotic asked as she parked beside a white Pathfinder.

"Not at all, honey. You were once a detective and if you say we was being tailed, then that's what it was. Sunami used to always tell me, never second guess or underestimate your enemy."

After purchasing two sodas and a pack of Newport's, the women exited the store and looked cautiously for the black Yukon. They climbed into Sunami's Mercedes and pulled out into the light traffic. As they headed toward the West End, the Yukon appeared out of nowhere. Hypnotic saw but continued driving as if she hadn't taken notice. She made a left turn.

The Yukon continued to follow. Ms. Story told her to make a left turn onto James Street. The Yukon made the same turn. She then turned right and made another left turn. The Yukon trailed them at a distance but continued to follow.

Hypnotic quickly made another turn and floored the accelerator. Ms. Story dialed a number on her cell phone.

Hypnotic didn't see the Yukon in her rearview mirror. She sped down the street and made a right onto Lakewood.

The Yukon stopped abruptly ahead of them and Hypnotic sped right past the truck. The driver of the Yukon attempted to make a U-turn.

"Stop a minute!" Ms. Story advised. Hypnotic stopped the car and looked at Ms. Story. She was confused and about to speak. Ms. Story hushed her and told her to watch. She shifted in the seat and looked back to the Yukon.

Suddenly, the SUV was cut off by nine three-wheeled T-Rex vehicles. The Yukon driver honked furiously at the T-Rex crew, as they drove around and blocked his path.

Hypnotic laughed hysterically. "You called them, didn't you?"

"Sure did. Sumani and Shadow bought those for them when they graduated from school. He calls them the T-Rex crew. Them fellas love him to death."

The women's conversation came to an abrupt halt when she saw the driver get out of the Yukon. Hypnotic couldn't believe who it was stepping out. "Oh my god! Look!"

Chapter 22

Sunami stepped out of the shower and dried himself off. He then brushed his teeth and went into his bedroom and got dressed in gray sweatpants and a t-shirt. While tying his sneakers, he tried not to think about what was stated on the 6 o'clock news.

He paced the floor and constantly thought about how he was going to get Brianna back home. He only had one day left. As he sat down on the bed, Hypnotic and Ms. Story burst into the room.

"What's wrong? What happened?" he asked them.

Both women walked over and sat down on his bed.

"When we left Cuba's place, we were followed," Hypnotic began.

"What? By who?"

"At first, I didn't know. They were driving a black Yukon."

"They followed us to the End," Ms. Story cut in.

"What the hell y'all doing at the End?"

"Because I told Hypnotic to lead them there. Figured we had a better chance of shaking them."

"And?!"

"Thanks to those guys you bought those T-Rexes for, they cut them off," said Hypnotic.

"Damn! That's Shadow's cousin and little homies. They aight?"

"Yeah, they left when we got away. But guess who was following us."

"Who, Cuba?"

"No, baby. It was Amil!"

"Damn, how she get on you like that? What did you do?" He was suddenly worried even more about Brianna.

"We went out and found Cuba's estate, like you and I agreed on. I snuck onto his property and checked things out. I also took pictures."

"You know she's gonna tell him about you! And when she does…"

"She's not going to tell him anything! She doesn't have anything to tell him. That damn girl ain't never seen me before. So, what can she tell?"

Ms. Story stood to her feet. "She's right. Cuba has armed men all around that place. If she was spotted, they would've stopped her, not just one lone bimbo."

"She was following y'all for some reason. She wasn't behind y'all for nothing, that's for sure."

"If Cuba thought we was on to him like that, Mario would've called you by now and let you know that we fucked up. Amil probably thought I was some woman stalking Cuba. Let's just stick to the plan. When Mario calls tomorrow, tell him we got the money in cash and find out where he wants to meet, then we move in."

Sunami thought the plan was crazy. She first wanted everyone to pair in groups to break up Cuba's defense with distraction.

She printed the photos of Cuba's estate she had taken earlier with her digital camera. She and Douglas looked over them carefully and came up with a plan that would get them inside.

The night was getting late and Sunami told Hypnotic that he and Shadow would be up most of the night making moves, a few calls, and getting a few things from well-connected friends. He explained to her that he had a few tricks up his sleeve.

There was a knock at his door. "Come in!" he yelled.

Shadow entered the room with a face that spoke death. Sunami knew the look and realized that they had lost a soldier.

"My man called and told me Everlyn and Passion dead, son!"

"What?" Sunami yelled. "How?"

"My man said she and Passion had a shootout with Denise after they killed Kasara. Then Denise killed herself."

"Damn!" Sunami studied Shadow's face. Hypnotic excused herself so they could talk. "You gonna be alright?"

"I don't see why not. Worries and tears never brought back the dead."

"I like that. Spoken like a true soldier. You think that shit could lead back to us?"

"Nah. Me and Douglas hit 'em with stolen guns and gave them a stolen car. Besides, nobody down here knows them anyway. And that bitch Passion stayed in so much shit, the police ain't gonna sweat her being dead. You know we gotta kill Bullet now, cause if the police question him, that nigga gonna talk."

"You think so?"

"Shit, it's better safe than sorry with fed time."

Sunami's cell phone rang. "Hello."

"Yeah, who am I speaking with?" the caller asked.

"Sunami. Who is this?"

"Mr. Sunami, we finally get to speak."

"My daughter still alive?"

"You got my four million dollars?"

"Yeah, I do. And how would you like it delivered?"

"Good, good. To answer your question, I'm Cuba Sanchez. Yeah, your daughter is still alive. Just be glad I didn't send her ass to Cuba. You know they like young pussy down there."

"You sick bitch! If you—"

"No need for threats. You just meet me at midnight at the entrance of my estate." Cuba gave Sunami the address. "Bring the money and we'll conduct business. One minute late, she dies... understand?"

"Sure!" Sunami responded. He was boiling inside. "How do I know she's still alive?"

There was a moment of silence. "Daddy?"

"Brianna!"

"When you coming to get me?"

"Tonight, sweetheart."

"Daddy—" The phone went silent.

"Hello? Hello...hello," Sunami shouted repeatedly at the silence on the phone.

They all gathered in the living room and discussed the final details of the surprise attack.

Keese

Chapter 23

Twenty-five Heavy Infantry members dressed in black army combat fatigues encircled a long table. On this table was a large assortment of guns and weaponry for hand-to-hand combat. Each man stood ready to fight to their death. As they patiently waited for Hypnotic, the men casually conversed among each other like a small platoon before going to war.

Hypnotic came into the room and all eyes turned to her. Mouths dropped open because they couldn't believe how she was dressed. Her hair was gathered in a ponytail and somehow, she'd squeezed her full breasts, thick thighs, wide hips, and tight bubble ass into Sunami's extra black fatigues. Everyone was mesmerized by the African Amazon.

"Damn! Can you walk in that shit?" Sunami asked, eyeing her thick thighs, narrow waist, and the diamond-shaped gap between her legs. He sensed they were all undressing her with their eyes.

She blushed with a naughty gleam in her eyes and slowly walked to him, seductively swaying her hips as she took measured steps. She stopped only inches before him, smiled, and whispered in his ear, "When I get your daughter and we get back home, I'ma clean your gun, oil it, and let you do all the shooting you want." She cast a spell on him, hoping it would encourage him to come back home alive.

"Now that's for sho," he responded as everyone wondered what she whispered.

"Damn, Sunami, how many guns do you own?" she asked, looking at the table.

"About a hundred. My father, Papa Red, used to collect them. As I got older, I did the same. He's the one who taught us how to use them and how to fight before he died."

"Wow! You got everything too." She picked up an Uzi. She extended the stock, palmed the bolt back, and pulled the trigger to see where it broke before clicking.

"This is an Uzi Gal Type A, good weapon. It's steady and only weighs twelve pounds, and you can conceal it under a coat with a strap over the shoulder."

She placed the gun back on the table while eyeing the others. "You got some fine shit here. Colt AR-15, Beretta AR-70, Norinco Mac 90, Striker 12 Street Sweeper, 9mm Calico, AK-47, Tec-9 and M-1. American soldiers in World War II used those. They shoot a 7.62 mm bullet and they're accurate up to twelve yards."

"Damn, you know guns like that?" Sunami was impressed.

"Yeah, my dad taught me all I know."

"Well, how 'bout explaining those while I go handle something. We only used the smoke bangs. They're new and I haven't shown the others how to use them yet."

She reached across the table and took the black canisters in her hand then explained to the others how they worked. She looked around and could tell some of them weren't ready for such a responsibility. However, they were all devoted to Sunami and there was nothing she could say to change their minds.

She glanced at her watch. It was nearing 10:30 p.m.

She suggested they get ready. She took a brief moment to explain the effects of the shooting to get them all to understand that they soon would be fighting a battle that would require tactics, leadership, and the elimination of every threat. She also warned them to never overestimate their own abilities and to never underestimate the enemies.

She asked if anyone wanted to reconsider going on the mission. They all looked at her as if she was crazy.

"So, everyone's ready?" she asked, just as Sunami entered the room. Silently, they nodded their heads.

"Ain't nothing else to talk about then. Let's do it!" Shadow yelled as he looked at Sunami.

They all began loading equipment into the Hummers. Hypnotic walked over to her brother with her arms folded across her chest and a look of worry on her face. "You know you don't have to do this, Douglas."

"Yeah, you don't either, sis," Douglas responded.

There was a moment of silence. "We're doing this for Brianna," she said and hugged her brother.

They met Sunami at the door. "You, okay?" he asked.

"Yeah." They stared into each other's eyes, not knowing what to say.

"Hypnotic, I love you and appreciate all the help you've given me."

They both walked slowly, hand in hand, to his Hummer. Neither spoke a word. He turned and gently caressed her face with his fingertip, then slowly leaned in and kissed her passionately.

"You sure you can handle that thing?" he asked, handing her the helmet for the motorcycle.

"Watch me!"

"Be careful, and remember all you do is get her out once I call you in. Then y'all get on that bike and ride like hell. Your brother strapped her helmet to the seat."

"Yes, daddy! Sunami, I love you. If you don't come back to me, I'ma kill you...you hear?"

"Yeah." Suddenly his face went blank. "Listen, I called my attorney two days ago. Contact him if anything happens to me and Shadow."

"Baby, please, don't talk like that. We need you, both of us."

He jumped into his truck and drove off. She mounted the bike and followed behind the entourage of killers.

Keese

Chapter 24

A silver Lincoln with darkened windows stopped before the tall entry gates of Cuba Sanchez's estate. The windows lowered slowly. A guard dressed in a black suit approached. The guard spoke briefly with the driver and waved him through seconds later.

The car slowly entered and traveled down the black road that was lit by the moon. A six-foot-one Cuban with thinning hair in a dark suit surveyed the premises as the car neared him.

The Lincoln came to a complete stop. A husky man got out of the car and walked in front of the mansion. He approached the door and spoke to the guard posted under a light, nodded his head, and entered. The guard never spoke a word, and his ruthless face showed no expression.

Five minutes later, three more cars entered the estate. The man who exited the first car was holding a briefcase. He walked to the back and opened the door and spoke a few words as the driver ran around to meet him.

The driver reached in and pulled a little girl form the back seat. The girl kicked and screamed. She tried to bite the man, but was slapped by the woman who got out of the second car. The child had tears in her eyes.

"That son of a bitch!" Sunami said in anger. "I'ma kills that motherfucker, for real!"

Hypnotic heard him through the communication device and told him to remain focused and not let his anger get to him.

"When do we move in on them?" Black asked.

"Hold your position," advised Hypnotic. "We can't move in right now, but as soon as I receive word that Cuba's place has been shot up, some of his men will leave to go investigate. Then we'll move in. Not until then."

Heavy Infantry had taken concealment in the darkness of the woods around Cuba's mansion. At 11:45 p.m., Hypnotic received word that Cuba's place had been hit. Less than sixty seconds later, six men ran out of the house, jumped into cars, and raced through the gates, leaving the compound.

"Mr. Sanchez, everything okay, sir?" asked the guard posted under the light.

"Not sure yet. Some cock breath shot up my business. Come inside, I need you to watch the girl. I shouldn't be long."

"Sure, boss!"

Seconds later, three large Dobermans ran outside.

Hypnotic never spoke of seeing dogs when she briefed everyone. The dogs sniffed the ground, and Sunami puckered his lips and began making kissing sounds to call the puppies to play. The dogs raised their heads and sprinted toward the edge of the woods to meet their death. Sunami raised his 9 mm equipped with a silencer and took aim. Three shots whispered in the dark, turning the dogs into hushpuppies. Sunami and two others dragged the dog's feet first into the woods.

One of the guards asked his partner if he heard something. When his partner stated that the dogs were probably chasing some stray cat, he decided to investigate. He strolled past Black, unaware of the killer hiding behind the tree.

"Take him out!" Sunami whispered to Black.

Black removes his knife and crouched low to the ground. He jumped on the guard's back and wrapped his forearm around his throat. The guard squeezed and strained to breathe. He grabbed his attacker's arm and shook wildly in an attempt to fling him back.

Black wrestled the man to the ground and put the knife against the man's neck and opened his throat like a mouth. Blood gushed out onto his hands. He then slid the knife across his pant leg, wiping it free of the man's blood before placing it back in its scabbard, and then dragged the dead body into the woods.

When the guard's partner hadn't returned, he grew weary and pulled his weapon before going to see what was happening. He scanned the compound as he walked. He saw nothing and called his partner's name three times. There was no answer.

Shadow responded to the guard's call with a deadly silencer that coughed twice. The man's head snapped violently back before he dropped to the ground.

After both guards were taken down, Hypnotic ordered Heavy Infantry to move in on the house. They moved silently through the wood and hustled across the grass. As they neared, things suddenly went wrong. Motion lights positioned on the house kicked in, illuminating the property. Armed men appeared out of nowhere, scrambling around to protect their boss from attack.

One of the guard's Uzi spits and cut down five members of the Heavy Infantry. Shadow dove to the ground beside Sunami and switched his MP5 to fully automatic.

Men yelled from both sides as bullets whizzed through the air, killing and wounding all in their path. The scene was chaotic and bloody.

Sunami held down on his trigger and his targets lost their heads in plugs of misty blood. Hypnotic informed Sunami that she was going in for Brianna. He feared that he would lose them both and tried to convince her that it was too dangerous. They had no idea how many armed men were inside. However, she refused to listen.

Hypnotic sprinted toward the house. She feared that Brianna was already dead. She cursed herself for not checking for the motion sensor lights. She stopped at the side entrance of the mansion and looked around for cameras. She saw several and realized the situation called for more than just gun power. She shot out all the surrounding lights. When she shot out the last light, she called out to Sunami.

When he responded, she smiled. Sunami and Hypnotic entered the house. Black, Douglas, and Scar covered the rear as they followed behind. Sunami called Shadow through the communication device. When he heard no response, he feared he had lost his best friend. He stopped to put his back against the wall and found he felt weak.

"This is not the time to quit, Sunami. We came to do a job. If we don't, there's a good chance your little girl could die," said Hypnotic.

"So right you are," said a thundering voice from down the hall. "Just look at you, you piece of shit!"

Sunami raised his head and saw that Cuba had a gun flush to Brianna's head. Standing beside Cuba was Amil holding a gun.

With the reflex, strength, speed, and apprehension of cops, Hypnotic and Douglas quickly aimed their weapons at Cuba and Amil.

"Drop your weapons!" Hypnotic shouted. "Both of you, now!"

Cuba looked her in the eyes with the intensity of a laser. He then cocked back the hammer of the gun he was holding to the little girl's head. "Let me get this straight. You want me to drop my gun? Is that what you're telling me?" Cuba asked and suddenly shot Douglas in the chest.

Douglas dropped to the floor, gasping for air and looking at his sister. Sunami went to him and noticed a massive hole in his vest. He lowered his ear to Douglas's mouth and told Hypnotic that he was dead.

"Motherfuckers got KTW cop killers!" Sunami yelled, warning everyone. Cuba was using Teflon-coated bullets designed to shoot through a cop's vest.

"Look at this face, bitch!" Sunami said as he pulled his helmet off. "Because when I kill you, I want you to tell God I sent you!"

"Daddy, shoot him, shoot him!" Brianna yelled.

The tension in the air was a physical force.

Hypnotic could not let her brother's death cloud her judgment. "You win," she said and dropped her gun to the floor. She then whispered into the communication device,

"On my signal, I want you all to pull flash bangs." The others also dropped their guns.

"You people always like to kill others, but you're never willing to die in return," said Cuba. "Now, let's move."

As Cuba led them to the back room at gunpoint, Sunami slid on his helmet to communicate with the others. Cuba was unaware that they were all communicating.

"In there!" Cuba shouted. "As you see, my floor is covered in plastic because we knew you were coming. You see, my beautiful daughter over here spotted your lady friend snooping around today. We would've killed the bitch, but she got away from us."

174

"You!" said Amil. "Remove your helmet. Let me see your face."

Hypnotic slowly removed her helmet and looked the woman in the eyes. Amil walked over to Hypnotic and kissed her on the mouth. Slowly, Hypnotic kissed the woman back as their tongues danced and snaked around in each other's mouth.

"You kiss very well. It's a shame I have to kill you," said Amil. She then slapped Hypnotic across the face with her gun. "Over there, now move!" she ordered, motioning her with the gun.

Hypnotic walked slowly past the window. She had to think of something. "Before you kill me, can I have one more kiss...please?" she asked, stalling for time to think.

Amil thought that Hypnotic was attempting to change her mind in order to spare her life. She decided, what the hell, one kiss wouldn't hurt. Slowly, she walked over to Hypnotic and kissed her passionately.

Black saw a moment to run and broke for the door.

Cuba was caught off guard and couldn't decide to chase him or stay. Amil told him to go and he quickly chased Black. The moment he entered the hall, shots rang out loudly from his gun.

As they all stood in silence, being held at bay by Amil's gun, Hypnotic looked around the room for reasons she didn't even know. All of a sudden, Shadow peeked through the door, holding a flash bang. Amil and the others had no idea he was even there.

"In five seconds," Hypnotic said loud enough for Shadow to hear. "I'ma take your dike ass out, you bad breath bitch."

Amil laughed wildly and called her crazy. As she laughed, Hypnotic told them to cover their ears and close their eyes because she didn't want them to witness the ass kicking, she was about to unleash. No one understood what Hypnotic was talking about, but knew she had a trick up her sleeve. When Brianna failed to cover her eyes and ears, Sunami told her it was okay and not to open them until Hypnotic said so.

A few seconds later, a black canister rolled into the room. Amil looked at the canister, perplexed. Just as she bent down to pick it up, it exploded with a blinding light and deafening noise. She dropped to the floor, screaming as if she had suffered a concussion.

Hypnotic rushed her and began punching her with a combination of jabs, breaking her nose, busting her lip, and cracking jaw.

"Help! Help!" someone yelled in the hallway.

Hypnotic ran to the hall. "Oh my god! Can you stand up and walk?" she asked Shadow.

Shadow had been shot in the leg and lower stomach and had lost a lot of blood. "Yeah, but shit, I'm weak. Look, there goes my baby. You okay, sweetheart?"

Brianna kneeled down beside Shadow and hugged him with tears in her eyes. "Thank you, Uncle Shadow."

As Sunami and Hypnotic helped Shadow up, Cuba rounded the corner holding a gun. He shot Scar in the neck and he died instantly.

"Hold it right there or the little black bitch will get the next one!" Cuba yelled.

Shadow removed his hands from around Sunami's and Hypnotic's necks to stand on his own. "Y'all get behind me, bro," he said to Sunami. "Only if your Cuban ass go through me first."

Shadow lifted his jacket and exposed the 9mm tucked in his back. He then limped forward and grabbed Brianna and spun as Sunami simultaneously snatched the gun from Shadow's holster.

Cuba let off two shots as Hypnotic dove to the floor. Shadow held Brianna in his arms and took two slugs intended for her in his back. As he fell down on top of her, shielding her, Sunami pumped six shots dead center into Cuba's chest.

"Y'all get out of here. I'll get Shadow," Sunami yelled as Brianna stood up. Hypnotic stared at him as she stood to her feet. "Go! I'll be home!" he yelled. "I can't leave Shadow like this, baby."

The moment she and Brianna left the house, she spotted headlights moving fast up the road. She was about to go back for Sunami, but realized there wasn't time. As they entered the woods, she paused to see who was heading toward the house. She then gasped as the cop cars, ambulances, and SWAT pulled up.

Brianna called out for her daddy over and over with tears in her eyes. Hypnotic promised her that her daddy would be home. She prayed she was right.

As Sunami tossed Shadow over his shoulder, he noticed headlights shining through the window. When SWAT entered the house, he dropped Shadow and ran and tossed four flash bang grenades. He then opens fired and tried to kill as many as he could, knowing he didn't have much time. When SWAT realized they were being ambushed, they ran back outside to regroup.

Chapter 25

Sunami woke up before sunrise. He rolled over and looked at his digital clock. "Damn!" he said as he noticed the time was 5:48 a.m. He lay awake, staring at the ceiling with nothing on his mind as his wife slept with her chin nestled in the fold of his arm. Her soft skin felt heavenly to him.

"Morning," she whispered with a lewd sparkle in her brown eyes. "Whatcha doing up so early?" she asked, grabbing his erection and nibbling on his ear.

"I was laying here, thinking of you and Brianna."

He noticed her smile.

She began slithering her tongue down the length of his stomach, setting him ablaze as every nerve in his body awoke to the sensation. As her lips neared his erection, he dumbly asked, "What are you doing?"

She stopped and raised her head. "Getting breakfast in bed. You denying me a meal?"

He groaned with pleasure as she kissed the stiffness of his head. The sight of her long hair spread over his stomach heightened his pleasure. She continued taking him in, inch by inch, into her warm mouth. After nearly ten minutes of nonstop pleasure, his erection stiffened even harder. He clenched the bed sheets and arched his hips upward. She sensed him nearing a powerful orgasm. She suddenly stopped, rolled over on her back and opened her legs. "Put it in me before she wakes up, baby."

He slowly pressed into her warm slit. She arched her back and gasped as her pussy slowly stretched to fit his enormous size.

He stroked her deeper with a steady rhythm as her body began to shudder. "Oh god, oooh, uuumm," she cried.

She then raised her legs and locked them around his neck. His shaft penetrated her deeper and she could now feel him in her stomach. As his hot liquid filled her pussy, she yelled loudly. Her vagina muscles contracted against his erection as they came simultaneously.

"What the," he yelled, as they scrambled to cover themselves with the sheets.

"Daddy, I'm hungry," Brianna said, bursting through the door into the room. "Can Nanna make me some pancakes? She cooks better than you do."

"Oh, she does, huh?" he said, playfully jumping to his feet with the sheets wrapped around him. Hypnotic burst out laughing as Brianna ran around the large bed giggling. He playfully tossed her up on the bed and tickled her. "So, she cooks better than me, huh?"

Brianna screamed and laughed at the same time. "Yeah, and she cooks better than Mommy too."

Sunami suddenly felt like he had been punched. He stopped and sat on the side of the bed, thinking of Brittany. He actually missed all their fighting.

Hypnotic sensed his pain and slid closer to him from behind, resting her chin on his shoulder and hugging him around the waist.

The three of them talked about Brittany for a few minutes. "I miss her, Daddy, but at least she's happier now!" Brianna said. "Heaven is everybody's home. Only God can call you there."

"Who told you that, baby girl?" Sunami asked her.

"Mommy did!" she responded, referring to Hypnotic. "She said we gonna go one day. I don't understand a lot of it, but I know God loves us," she said and hugged her daddy. "And soon I'll have a little brother."

Brianna soon realized her slip of the tongue and covered her mouth.

Sunami turned slowly to Hypnotic. "You pregnant, honey?"

"Yes! Six weeks. I wanted to surprise you," she replied.

Sunami danced around with the sheet, jumped around the bed and ran to the mirror. "We pregnant! Woooo!" he yelled and jumped into the bed. "Why didn't you tell me sooner?"

"Because I wanted to wait until after we go see Shadow and my brother today."

"Damn, today is Shadow's birthday. Can't believe he's been gone for almost six months."

"Me either. Don't forget, you're supposed to tell me how you got away. You promised to tell me today."

"Tell me too!" Brianna said.

"I will. It's time I talk about it," he admitted.

They all showered, dressed, ate breakfast, and then drove to the cemetery. They approached Shadow's grave with sorrow and wished things had turned out differently.

"Uncle Shadow, I miss you," said Brianna. "We all miss you. And guess what? I'ma be a big sister soon!" She smiled. "I love you, Shadow."

Hypnotic stepped forward and glanced at the flowers she was holding. "Hey there, big fella. Really don't know what to say, but I guess it's best to say what I feel. We really didn't get to know one another as well as we should have. You were taken too soon, and that hurts like hell," she said, looking at Brianna. "But I understand…as a matter of fact, we all do. I know you were a true friend for life. You saved our lives, especially this little girl here, and she never stops talking about you. We all miss your crazy ass," she said as she placed the flowers on the grave.

Sunami stepped forward and looked up to the sky. He held his hands out to his side. "Lord, please bless this thug."

After a moment of silence, Sunami spoke again.

"This is the first time I've been here since the funeral. Damn near all of Durham came out. But now that I'm back, I'ma tell you what I didn't say then, homey. When you gave your life to save Brianna's, I told Hypnotic to take her home. When they left, I searched Cuba's office and found the disk he had of you and Everlyn. So, when I got ready to leave with you on my shoulder, I saw the police coming. Once they came into the house, I opened fire on all of them with all I had, knowing I was gonna die. But they left, word! I disfigured two dead officers' faces, undressed you and me, and put their clothes on us and dressed them in our Heavy Infantry clothes. The second time they came in, stupid niggas didn't even know the difference. I walked out with you on my shoulder and got into the ambulance. On the way to the hospital, I killed them all."

He drew in a deep breath, trying to control his emotions.

"Now I'm here telling you, thanks for a lifetime of sincere brotherhood. Thanks for giving your life so Brianna, Hypnotic, and I can carry on with ours. You'll always live through us."

Keese

To Be Continued…
Hood Consigliere 2
Coming Soon

Lock Down Publications and Ca$h Presents assisted publishing packages.

BASIC PACKAGE $499
Editing
Cover Design
Formatting

UPGRADED PACKAGE $800
Typing
Editing
Cover Design
Formatting

ADVANCE PACKAGE $1,200
Typing
Editing
Cover Design
Formatting
Copyright registration
Proofreading
Upload book to Amazon

LDP SUPREME PACKAGE $1,500
Typing
Editing
Cover Design
Formatting
Copyright registration
Proofreading
Set up Amazon account
Upload book to Amazon
Advertise on LDP Amazon and Facebook page

***Other services available upon request. Additional
charges may apply
**Lock Down Publications
P.O. Box 944
Stockbridge, GA 30281-9998
Phone # 470 303-9761**

Submission Guideline

Submit the first three chapters of your completed manuscript to ldpsubmissions@gmail.com, subject line: Your book's title. The manuscript must be in a .doc file and sent as an attachment. Document should be in Times New Roman, double spaced and in size 12 font. Also, provide your synopsis and full contact information. If sending multiple submissions, they must each be in a separate email.

Have a story but no way to send it electronically? You can still submit to LDP/Ca$h Presents. Send in the first three chapters, written or typed, of your completed manuscript to:

LDP: Submissions Dept
Po Box 944
Stockbridge, Ga 30281

DO NOT send original manuscript. Must be a duplicate.

Provide your synopsis and a cover letter containing your full contact information.

Thanks for considering LDP and Ca$h Presents.

NEW RELEASES

FOR THE LOVE OF BLOOD by JAMEL MITCHELL
CONCRETE KILLA 3 by KINGPEN
RAN OFF ON DA PLUG by PAPER BOI RARI
THE BRICK MAN 4 by KING RIO
HOOD CONSIGLIERE by KEESE

Hood Consigliere

Coming Soon from Lock Down Publications/Ca$h Presents

BLOOD OF A BOSS **VI**

SHADOWS OF THE GAME II

TRAP BASTARD II

By **Askari**

LOYAL TO THE GAME **IV**

By **T.J. & Jelissa**

IF TRUE SAVAGE **VIII**

MIDNIGHT CARTEL IV

DOPE BOY MAGIC IV

CITY OF KINGZ III

NIGHTMARE ON SILENT AVE II

THE PLUG OF LIL MEXICO II

By **Chris Green**

BLAST FOR ME **III**

A SAVAGE DOPEBOY III

CUTTHROAT MAFIA III

DUFFLE BAG CARTEL VII

HEARTLESS GOON VI

By **Ghost**

A HUSTLER'S DECEIT III

KILL ZONE II

BAE BELONGS TO ME III

By **Aryanna**

KING OF THE TRAP III

By **T.J. Edwards**

GORILLAZ IN THE BAY V

3X KRAZY III

STRAIGHT BEAST MODE II

De'Kari

187

Keese

KINGPIN KILLAZ IV

STREET KINGS III

PAID IN BLOOD III

CARTEL KILLAZ IV

DOPE GODS III

Hood Rich

SINS OF A HUSTLA II

ASAD

RICH $AVAGE II

By Martell Troublesome Bolden

YAYO V

Bred In The Game 2

S. Allen

CREAM III

THE STREETS WILL TALK II

By Yolanda Moore

SON OF A DOPE FIEND III

HEAVEN GOT A GHETTO II

By Renta

LOYALTY AIN'T PROMISED III

By Keith Williams

I'M NOTHING WITHOUT HIS LOVE II

SINS OF A THUG II

TO THE THUG I LOVED BEFORE II

IN A HUSTLER I TRUST II

By Monet Dragun

QUIET MONEY IV

EXTENDED CLIP III

THUG LIFE IV

By **Trai'Quan**

Hood Consigliere

THE STREETS MADE ME IV

By **Larry D. Wright**

IF YOU CROSS ME ONCE II

By **Anthony Fields**

THE STREETS WILL NEVER CLOSE IV

By **K'ajji**

HARD AND RUTHLESS III

KILLA KOUNTY III

By Khufu

MONEY GAME III

By Smoove Dolla

JACK BOYS VS DOPE BOYS II

A GANGSTA'S QUR'AN V

COKE GIRLZ II

By Romell Tukes

MURDA WAS THE CASE II

Elijah R. Freeman

THE STREETS NEVER LET GO II

By Robert Baptiste

AN UNFORESEEN LOVE III

By **Meesha**

KING OF THE TRENCHES III

by **GHOST & TRANAY ADAMS**

MONEY MAFIA II

LOYAL TO THE SOIL III

By **Jibril Williams**

QUEEN OF THE ZOO II

By **Black Migo**

VICIOUS LOYALTY III

By Kingpen

Keese

A GANGSTA'S PAIN III

By J-Blunt

CONFESSIONS OF A JACKBOY III

By Nicholas Lock

GRIMEY WAYS II

By Ray Vinci

KING KILLA II

By Vincent "Vitto" Holloway

BETRAYAL OF A THUG II

By Fre$h

THE MURDER QUEENS II

By Michael Gallon

THE BIRTH OF A GANGSTER II

By Delmont Player

TREAL LOVE II

By Le'Monica Jackson

FOR THE LOVE OF BLOOD II

By Jamel Mitchell

RAN OFF ON DA PLUG II

By Paper Boi Rari

HOOD CONSIGLIERE II

By Keese

Hood Consigliere

Keese

BORN HEARTLESS I II III IV

KING OF THE TRAP I II

By **T.J. Edwards**

IF LOVING HIM IS WRONG…I & II

LOVE ME EVEN WHEN IT HURTS I II III

By **Jelissa**

WHEN THE STREETS CLAP BACK I & II III

THE HEART OF A SAVAGE I II III

MONEY MAFIA

LOYAL TO THE SOIL I II

By **Jibril Williams**

A DISTINGUISHED THUG STOLE MY HEART I II & III

LOVE SHOULDN'T HURT I II III IV

RENEGADE BOYS I II III IV

PAID IN KARMA I II III

SAVAGE STORMS I II III

AN UNFORESEEN LOVE I II

By **Meesha**

A GANGSTER'S CODE I &, II III

A GANGSTER'S SYN I II III

THE SAVAGE LIFE I II III

CHAINED TO THE STREETS I II III

BLOOD ON THE MONEY I II III

A GANGSTA'S PAIN I II

By **J-Blunt**

PUSH IT TO THE LIMIT

By **Bre' Hayes**

BLOOD OF A BOSS **I, II, III, IV, V**

SHADOWS OF THE GAME

TRAP BASTARD

Hood Consigliere

By **Askari**
THE STREETS BLEED MURDER **I, II & III**
THE HEART OF A GANGSTA I II& III
By **Jerry Jackson**
CUM FOR ME I II III IV V VI VII VIII
An **LDP Erotica Collaboration**
BRIDE OF A HUSTLA **I II & II**
THE FETTI GIRLS **I, II& III**
CORRUPTED BY A GANGSTA I, II III, IV
BLINDED BY HIS LOVE
THE PRICE YOU PAY FOR LOVE I, II ,III
DOPE GIRL MAGIC I II III
By **Destiny Skai**
WHEN A GOOD GIRL GOES BAD
By **Adrienne**
THE COST OF LOYALTY I II III
By Kweli
A GANGSTER'S REVENGE **I II III & IV**
THE BOSS MAN'S DAUGHTERS I II III IV V
A SAVAGE LOVE **I & II**
BAE BELONGS TO ME I II
A HUSTLER'S DECEIT I, II, III
WHAT BAD BITCHES DO I, II, III
SOUL OF A MONSTER I II III
KILL ZONE
A DOPE BOY'S QUEEN I II III
By **Aryanna**
A KINGPIN'S AMBITON
A KINGPIN'S AMBITION **II**
I MURDER FOR THE DOUGH

Keese

By **Ambitious**
TRUE SAVAGE I II III IV V VI VII
DOPE BOY MAGIC I, II, III
MIDNIGHT CARTEL I II III
CITY OF KINGZ I II
NIGHTMARE ON SILENT AVE
THE PLUG OF LIL MEXICO II

By **Chris Green**
A DOPEBOY'S PRAYER
By **Eddie "Wolf" Lee**
THE KING CARTEL **I, II & III**
By **Frank Gresham**
THESE NIGGAS AIN'T LOYAL **I, II & III**
By **Nikki Tee**
GANGSTA SHYT **I II &III**
By **CATO**
THE ULTIMATE BETRAYAL
By **Phoenix**
BOSS'N UP **I , II & III**
By **Royal Nicole**
I LOVE YOU TO DEATH
By **Destiny J**
I RIDE FOR MY HITTA
I STILL RIDE FOR MY HITTA
By **Misty Holt**
LOVE & CHASIN' PAPER
By **Qay Crockett**
TO DIE IN VAIN
SINS OF A HUSTLA

194

Hood Consigliere

By **ASAD**
BROOKLYN HUSTLAZ
By **Boogsy Morina**
BROOKLYN ON LOCK I & II
By **Sonovia**
GANGSTA CITY
By **Teddy Duke**
A DRUG KING AND HIS DIAMOND I & II III
A DOPEMAN'S RICHES
HER MAN, MINE'S TOO I, II
CASH MONEY HO'S
THE WIFEY I USED TO BE I II
By Nicole Goosby
TRAPHOUSE KING **I II & III**
KINGPIN KILLAZ I II III
STREET KINGS I II
PAID IN BLOOD **I II**
CARTEL KILLAZ I II III
DOPE GODS I II
By **Hood Rich**
LIPSTICK KILLAH **I, II, III**
CRIME OF PASSION I II & III
FRIEND OR FOE I II III
By **Mimi**
STEADY MOBBN' **I, II, III**
THE STREETS STAINED MY SOUL I II III
By **Marcellus Allen**
WHO SHOT YA **I, II, III**
SON OF A DOPE FIEND I II
HEAVEN GOT A GHETTO

Keese

Renta
GORILLAZ IN THE BAY **I II III IV**
TEARS OF A GANGSTA I II
3X KRAZY I II
STRAIGHT BEAST MODE
DE'KARI
TRIGGADALE I II III
MURDAROBER WAS THE CASE
Elijah R. Freeman
GOD BLESS THE TRAPPERS I, II, III
THESE SCANDALOUS STREETS I, II, III
FEAR MY GANGSTA I, II, III IV, V
THESE STREETS DON'T LOVE NOBODY I, II
BURY ME A G I, II, III, IV, V
A GANGSTA'S EMPIRE I, II, III, IV
THE DOPEMAN'S BODYGAURD I II
THE REALEST KILLAZ I II III
THE LAST OF THE OGS I II III
Tranay Adams
THE STREETS ARE CALLING
Duquie Wilson
MARRIED TO A BOSS I II III
By Destiny Skai & Chris Green
KINGZ OF THE GAME I II III IV V VI
Playa Ray
SLAUGHTER GANG I II III
RUTHLESS HEART I II III
By Willie Slaughter
FUK SHYT
By Blakk Diamond

196

Hood Consigliere

DON'T F#CK WITH MY HEART I II

By Linnea

ADDICTED TO THE DRAMA I II III

IN THE ARM OF HIS BOSS II

By Jamila

YAYO I II III IV

A SHOOTER'S AMBITION I II

BRED IN THE GAME

By S. Allen

TRAP GOD I II III

RICH $AVAGE

MONEY IN THE GRAVE I II III

By Martell Troublesome Bolden

FOREVER GANGSTA

GLOCKS ON SATIN SHEETS I II

By Adrian Dulan

TOE TAGZ I II III IV

LEVELS TO THIS SHYT I II

By Ah'Million

KINGPIN DREAMS I II III

RAN OFF ON DA PLUG

By Paper Boi Rari

CONFESSIONS OF A GANGSTA I II III IV

CONFESSIONS OF A JACKBOY I II

By Nicholas Lock

I'M NOTHING WITHOUT HIS LOVE

SINS OF A THUG

TO THE THUG I LOVED BEFORE

A GANGSTA SAVED XMAS

IN A HUSTLER I TRUST

Keese

Hood Consigliere

IN THE BLINK OF AN EYE

By **Anthony Fields**

THE LIFE OF A HOOD STAR

By **Ca$h & Rashia Wilson**

THE STREETS WILL NEVER CLOSE I II III

By **K'ajji**

CREAM I II

THE STREETS WILL TALK

By **Yolanda Moore**

NIGHTMARES OF A HUSTLA I II III

By **King Dream**

CONCRETE KILLA I II III

VICIOUS LOYALTY I II

By **Kingpen**

HARD AND RUTHLESS I II

MOB TOWN 251

THE BILLIONAIRE BENTLEYS I II III

By **Von Diesel**

GHOST MOB

Stilloan Robinson

MOB TIES I II III IV V VI

By **SayNoMore**

BODYMORE MURDERLAND I II III

THE BIRTH OF A GANGSTER

By **Delmont Player**

FOR THE LOVE OF A BOSS

By **C. D. Blue**

MOBBED UP I II III IV

THE BRICK MAN I II III IV

THE COCAINE PRINCESS I II III IV V

Keese

By King Rio
KILLA KOUNTY I II III
By Khufu
MONEY GAME I II
By Smoove Dolla
A GANGSTA'S KARMA I II
By FLAME
KING OF THE TRENCHES I II
by GHOST & TRANAY ADAMS
QUEEN OF THE ZOO
By Black Migo
GRIMEY WAYS
By Ray Vinci
XMAS WITH AN ATL SHOOTER
By Ca$h & Destiny Skai
KING KILLA
By Vincent "Vitto" Holloway
BETRAYAL OF A THUG
By Fre$h
THE MURDER QUEENS
By Michael Gallon
TREAL LOVE
By Le'Monica Jackson
FOR THE LOVE OF BLOOD
By Jamel Mitchell
HOOD CONSIGLIERE
By Keese

BOOKS BY LDP'S CEO, CA$H

TRUST IN NO MAN

TRUST IN NO MAN 2

TRUST IN NO MAN 3

BONDED BY BLOOD

SHORTY GOT A THUG

THUGS CRY

THUGS CRY 2

THUGS CRY 3

TRUST NO BITCH

TRUST NO BITCH 2

TRUST NO BITCH 3

TIL MY CASKET DROPS

RESTRAINING ORDER

RESTRAINING ORDER 2

IN LOVE WITH A CONVICT

LIFE OF A HOOD STAR

XMAS WITH AN ATL SHOOTER

Keese

CPSIA information can be obtained
at www.ICGtesting.com
Printed in the USA
LVHW042034220822
726558LV00007B/44